ONE HUNDRED HOURS OF HOPE

a novel

Pascale Doxy

ONE HUNDRED HOURS OF HOPE

a novel

Translated from French by Garry F. Doxy

One Hundred Hours of Hope

Original publication : « *Cent Heures à l'Expo 49* »

ISBN: 979-8-218-94544-2

Printed in the USA by Lulu Press, Inc.

Historical novel by Pascale Doxy

HEIRS TO A CAUSE

Old pains are reasons to live.
The more hardship we face, the more we should give
in to ultimate aspirations, to dreams, to the luminescence
That float and comfort us in the world of essence...

Etzer Vilaire
Les Dix Hommes Noirs (The Ten Black Men)

CHAPTER 1
The Dreamer from the Town of Jérémie

A breeze from the Gulf of *La Gonâve* was cooling down the temperature in Port-au-Prince in this late January of 1950. Yet, a young man, Solon Férila, was drench, dripping wet. He removed his wide straw hat to fan his strong angular face. A hand on his hip, he took a dirty handkerchief from the back pocket of his faded brown pants to pat his forehead. The smell of the ocean teased the young man's nostrils; around where he stood, the flamboyant trees and giant palm trees beautified and shaded the area.

It had been barely a year since Solon Férila left the region of *Grand-Anse* for the capital. Since he arrived, he busied himself at various jobs: messenger, water seller, load carrier at the *Croix-des-Bossales* farmers' market. He had been one of those laborers who unloaded the countless cargo ships coming into Port-au-Prince's harbor, filled with wooden planks and stakes, scrap metal, and steel. All this material were being use to bring to life the various pavilions that were to immortalize the celebrations of the Bicentennial of the city of Port-au-Pince. Solon, in his servile job, followed intelligently the directions of the agronomists from the Department of Agriculture to transplant the many palm trees that were lining the Harry Truman Boulevard. He worked hard at all his endeavors including this gardening job at the *Palmistes.*

The young man closed his eyes, offering his face to the sun while breathing for a moment the salty air. He dropped his hat on the floor, put both hands at his back, bent backwards, and whispered an "ouch". He was in a bit of pain; fatigue and hunger were accentuating it. However, driven by his obsession of a work well done, he got on his knees and continued caring for the landscape.

Maintaining the various areas of the *Palmistes* garden was not his only job. Solon also painted houses and buildings. He was among those who put the finishing touches on the Tourism Palace. He painted the walls and ceilings so meticulously that the foreman offered him to carry out a more artistic work at the *Pavillon de la Petite Industrie* (Small Business Pavillion). Since that day, he searched for a so-called artistic job, but he did not find anything that pleased him. Being from *Jérémie,* he has the inner leaning of a poet. After all, wasn't it the town of famous Haitian poets and writers?

Solon heard approaching footsteps behind him. Without turning his head, he recognized they were those of Cherilus, a co-worker friend. As the latter did every day, at noon, when shadows are short, he came to signal the time for lunch break.

"Rosa brought our food," he said.

"I'm coming," Solon answered in a frustrated tone.

Cherilus frowned and slightly arched his back.

"This isn't how we work in the city; I keep on telling you, man! From time to time, you need to *kalewès* (slowing down in regards to work) to regain your strength!"

Solon looked at his friend's fattened stomach, despite him being only twenty-two years of age. He had a double chin, surely the result of these *kalewès* that were causing his friend to gain weight and keeping it.

"*Kalewès* is not a word I know," replied Solon as he was trying to perfectly trim a bush. "You can go. Tell Rosa I'll be coming soon to get my food."

Cherilus gave him a disapproving look. Solon was putting too much energy into the simplest of actions. Cherilus went back to those childhood days when Solon refused to play with the children who lived in the thatched-house community. He was the eldest child, a position he took very seriously. He only played if his parents urged him to do so…

With a frown on his forehead, Cherilus marveled at Solon's agility. A profuse sweat followed the contractions on his friend's arm and a pleasant smile adorned his lips. Cherilus shook his head and walked away silently.

Fifteen minutes passed when Solon finally straightened up. He stepped back to admire what he planted. They lined up like soldiers in front of the rows of pink oleanders. He grabbed his hat and he looked up at the palm trees. A few yellowish branches were desperately dangling.

"After I finish eating," he told them, "I will take care of you, my beauties!"

Solon gathered his landscaping tools and headed to a corner of the parc that was facing the sea; it was there that Rosa, the lady merchant, erected her stall. Rosa was almost finishing her distribution of polenta with red peas and *legim* (mashed seasoned cooked vegetables). She was assisted by Shilette, her eighteen-year-old daughter, and a nephew who was barely twelve. Rosa's mobile restaurant never stayed in one place. Since the construction on the waterfront boardwalk started two years earlier, she had the bright idea of touring work sites to feed the workers; her excellent cuisine earned her a solid reputation. Because of the greenery and the ocean view, the *Palmistes* area was Rosa's favorite spot to sell her food.

"You almost miss everything," she said to Solon reproachfully.

"Ah..." the young man replied. "I know you wouldn't do that to me."

Solon smiled, revealing his short pale-yellow teeth. He sniffed the smell of coconut milk emanating from the polenta and salivated at its creamy aroma.

"You know I love *gratin* (overcook bottom crust of a dish in a cast pot)," he continued. "You can put some on my plate."

Looking stern, Rosa poured two ladles full of polenta while her daughter was cutting a slice of avocado to put on the plate.

"Come on, Shilette," Solon said, almost complaining. "Cut me a better slice!"

"You want half the avocado then?" Rosa asked bluntly.

Rosa looked at Solon from head to toe. Like him and many other workers, she too came from the countryside. She and Shilette were from the southeast, more precisely from Cayes-Jacmel. The laborers on the site were from all regions of the country: the elevated areas of the Center, the southeast mountains and plains, the eastern border with the Dominican Republic. Some workers were from the Dominican Republic itself. But Rosa and her daughter have settled in the capital for some time now and had becoming cosmopolitans. They were not impressed by Solon and his antics. Rosa was fed up with this newcomer who always showed up at the end of the meal, who spouted demands, and who even devoured his food with indescribable speed so that he could return to "his work".

"If you want more avocado, take your *senk kòb* (a penny) and go buy it yourself!" spat Rosa.

The way Rosa curled her lips signaled to Solon that if he wanted to continue to be part of her clientele, it would be best for him to go away.

While this exchange was taking place, Shilette was humming a tune by Lumane Casimir, a popular singer as young as herself. The heat was getting to her. She was not as plump as her mother, but she was not skinny either. With dark smooth skin, her dimples appeared on both of her cheeks as she smiled at Solon's interaction with her mother.

Solon took the plate from Shilette's hand, fascinated by the young girl's beauty. An excerpt from a Creole poem he had long heard came to his mind: *"Syèl! Ala bèl moun!"* (Heavens! What a beautiful girl!)

Shilette looked down as if she heard this flattering verse. Her dimples became deeper, like every afternoon when at lunch time Solon's gaze lingered on her.

Inspite of himself, Solon moved away with his plate. He joined Cherilus and the other workers who were in the middle of an animated discussion concerning various events taking place in the city. Some were surprised by the floating casino anchored in the bay; others found the aquarium of tropical fish of singular interest; still others were talking about the performances of several foreign groups at the *Théâtre de Verdure.*

"I heard," said a worker, "that there's going to be a dance competition right here at the *Palmistes*. But first, you must register."

"Oh! That's why I saw them doing renovations at the Simbie Night Club," stated Cherilus.

"Exactly," said one of them with a strong Dominican accent. "I helped them install a radio transmitter while they were redoing the dance floor. They even added some party lights."

"And how much does the registration cost?" asked another worker.

"*One gourde* ($0.20 USD)."

"Oh no! Not me!" said a sexagenarian man from Cap-Haitian. "I'm not going to use my hard-earned money to participate in a dance competition! They won't find me gyrating my money away, when I only earn a modest living during the day…"

"But it's not without a reward!" cried out another worker. "The winner will receive the equivalent of $1,000 USD!"

"Which is 5,000 *gourdes*!" exclaimed Cherilus.

"So," retorted the sexagenarian worker, "if they were to give away 5,000 *gourdes*, you think they would give it to us? That's for the *gwo zouzoun* (the upper-class) of this country! They are not doing these things for us!"

Solon gazed vaguely at the group. While others focused on what seemed to him pointless details, the sound of the 5,000 *gourdes* were echoing loudly in his ears. How many dreams he could give life to! How many changes he would make in his life! One thing he would immediately change was the banana-leaf mat that he was sleeping on every night. It would alleviate the pain of his overworked body. He was already feeling the firmness and suppleness of a real mattress made of soft cotton...

Sitting on the ground and his back against a coconut

tree, he was bent over his plate, eating his polenta. The silly chatter irritated him and his peaceful intake of food.

"And why not? Why not us?" he finally asked confidently.

All heads turned towards him. He did not look at them.

"Isn't it for everybody that President Estimé built the *Bord-de-Mer* (waterfront area)," he continued.

Solon wiped his lips with his shirtsleeve. Eyes closed, he leaned his head back slightly against the trunk of the coconut tree, ignoring still his co-workers' surprised faces.

He breathed in the sea air. The sound of the waves crashing against the stone-built embankment came to his hears like the waves of the AM radio stations he used to listen to when he was living in Jérémie; like the news loops he heard a few years ago about the government's major projects. He did not understand everything at the time, but some words spoken by President Estimé struck a chord within him.

"It is important that we take actions that bring hope; actions that show accountable authorities, respecting essential human rights, acting for the happiness of all...," he remembered the stately voice said.

Solon wanted to experience this promised glint of happiness. He has been searching for it for years; he has been trying to catch it like a child chasing a loose kite. These 5,000 *gourdes* could be that unexpected gift, the opportunity to start a dignified life; the chance to find the happiness he dreamed of so much.

Solon's distant gaze amused Cherilus.

"It's a dance competition!" he exclaimed. "And I've never seen you dance."

"Oh, oh! In my village, I was known as *konpè kòk* (jim-dandy rooster)." Solon replied, puffing out his chest. "*Kongo* danse is my specialty."

Solon's reaction caused a burst of laughter among the workers. One of them stood up and pretended to dance with an imaginary partner while singing a popular lyric in Creole:

Carolina Cao,
Danse Kongo jouk kò m fè mwen mal o!
Danse Kongo, laye Kongo
Carolina Cao nèg nwè ti zorèy anraje!

(Carolina Acao,
Dance Kongo until you're exhausted!

Dance Kongo, spread the Kongo
Carolina Acao, men with little years are going mad!)

The laughter continued as the workers kept the beat by clapping. Solon pinched his lips and felt victimized by the collective mockery.

"They can all laugh at me for now," he thought. "But I know that one day it will be me who will laugh at them. They will be silenced just like all those who didn't want to believe in the dream the president had for the nation."

The young man looked around him. All this greenery, these giant palm trees, these flowering shrubs, this heavenly place that the whole world wanted to visit and where he was laboring with so much pride, were before only dirt, filth and misery. It was a place dotted with pitiable dwellings worse than the one he lived in with thirteen family members in the town of Jérémie. He realized this with his ears glued to the radio stations; he saw it on the face of Cherilus and of all those who, when they returned to the countryside, were telling the beautiful tales of city life.

Solon let out a sigh. If the will of one president was able to transform this place like this, then why his own determination could not also change his life? No, he did not come this far to joke around. He was going to achieve his dreams; he was going to attempt all he can with quiet dignity.

"Well, *konpè kòk,*" said one of the workers, "this festival will cost you 1 *gourde* to register."

Solon shrugged casually.

"I'll find it," he kept on repeating to himself the whole day. "I'll find it."

He was not sure how, since he only was earning *1.50 gourde* a day ($0.30 USD). And that 1.50 *gourde* was not even enough to cover all his expenses. After paying the rent to Cherilus's wife, or rather the tiny space for the banana-leaf mat in a corner of their hovel, after sending money to his parents every month, after feeding himself, Solon was always short of funds.

Therefore, each *gourde* wasted would quickly become a real sacrifice. But, has not Solon's entire life been nothing else then an existence of sacrifice? So, to earn those 5,000 *gourdes,* he will have to do more. He will have to cut back on sleep and even eat a little less. There were other gardeners in the *Palmistes* parc, but he was the fastest and best of them all. He devised that he could finish early the job of painting houses; then, he could work as load bearer for a little while; and then, at the very least reconsider that position of craftsman at the *Pavillon de la Petite Industrie* (Small Business Pavillion).

The rest of the afternoon, Solon's actions were mechanical; he was too busy mulling over all the odd jobs that could quickly bring him the registration's fee, but also the extra money he so desperately needed for his everyday expenses.

Like every afternoon, Solon and Cherilus agreed that whoever finished first would wait for the other at a waterfront rampart facing the Gulf of *La Gonâve.* Solon arrived first that day. A light breeze fanned his clothes. He was lost in the contemplation of the setting sun and thought it look like the promise of a better tomorrow.

This waterfront that took only two months to be built was the embodiment of this 'better tomorrow'. The eastern neighboring republic and surrounding islands were envious of this achievement. The engineering and planning of the works were quite ambitious. Thanks to backfilling, the city grew by a few kilometers and renewed itself. The gained real estate was transformed. Concrete modern structures replaced wooden buildings with rusty metal roofs, giving an impression of strength and grandeur.

From one of his pockets, Solon pulled out a copy of a newspaper that was covering the walls of Cherilus' home.

Since the day he copied it, he kept it closely on him. He looked at the copy and tried to smooth the wrinkles and the upturn corners. It reminded him that he too was now part of this progressive march towards social advancement. Through his work, he also was seizing the opportunity to prove to the rest of the world that this nation's people desire to produce, to create beauty, and to take its place in the world.

Deep in such thoughts, Solon did not notice Cherilus arriving. He jumped a little when his friend patted his back and understood he was ready to go home.

"Were you serious about participating in the competition?" Cherilus asked him as soon as they started to walk.

Solon took a deep breath and his response came out with an ethereal exhalation. He broke off the stem of a plant, brought half into his mouth, and chewed it for a moment while he threw the rest into the sea.

"Yes," he replied confidently. "I'll sign up."

"This isn't a solo dance. You need a partner. Who would you dance with?"

Solon did not know what to answer. He has been in the capital for a year now; but still, he did not have a female friend. His work was his focus. Even Cherilus had difficulty convincing him to take a day off. Thus, Solon knew very few women. He knew only four: his friend's wife, the owner of a shop in their neighborhood who occasionally sold various things to him on credit, and finally Rosa and her daughter.

Shilette…

Solon's face lit up by thoughts of the young girl. Her long slender neck, her rounded face, and her pouting mouth which hid her astonishingly white teeth and *gencives violettes* (lovely dark gum shade of people with high concentration of melanin). Her facial beauty was framed by well-formed limbs and curves.

Suddenly, Solon stopped walking and spat out the piece of thc stem.

"Shilette! She won't mind!" he shouted.

Cherilus burst out laughing.

"Rosa will cut off your head first!"

"What if I offer to share the money with her?" Solon hastily argued. "I'm about to win 5,000 *gourdes*!"

Indeed, it was the salary of several years of work that Solon would pocket in a few hours. Shilette was a pretty girl, but very young. What could she possibly need? 500 *gourdes* ($100 USD) of the amount would be enough to make her happy, Solon thought. And with the rest of the money, he could live comfortably.

He would no longer live in the slum of *La Saline*. He would move to one of the chic districts of the city like *Bas-Peu-de-Chose* or at least *Poste Marchand*. He would stop being a gardener at the waterfront. He would learn how to drive and become a private chauffeur of a wealthy family. In a short time, he could set up a small business selling the excellent coffee his parents were growing in his village; it would be known all over the capital. And then, since he knew how to read, write and count, he would look for a beautiful *Port-au-Princienne* and marry her.

Solon took a deep breath. Those 5,000 *gourdes* ($1,000 USD) were like manna from heaven. He set off again, almost skipping, invigorated by so many projects. The beauty of the gardens, the buildings, the statues that were embellishing the boardwalk, seemed even more appealing to him. The smell of succulent food coming from many surrounding restaurants made him salivated. He stopped at a particularly lively restaurant. Solon gazed longingly through the large bay window.

"Rond-Point Café - Restaurant," he read to himself.

Now he could allow himself to think about the little pleasures of life, like eating in that restaurant. And one day, he will cross the front door...

CHAPTER 2
The Gentlemen from Bois-Verna

Rond-Point Café-Restaurant was standing proudly at a corner of the roundabout of Harry Truman Boulevard. The owner's cheerfulness and the house's specialty, the flambéed lobster, earned them a reputation among both locals and foreign visitors.

The decor of this spacious restaurant was simple but appealing. The inside resembled a large wine cave that kept the patrons cool. The massive walls felt like a fortress one retreats to when one needs to replenish their mind, their inner self. Large semicircular bay window meticulous cleaned, adorned the front of the restaurant, reducing the noise from the street for the patrons and offered to the passersby of all ages a vibrant and stimulating facade. It was the favorite spot for two regulars: Christian Grégoire and his best friend Augustin Montrose.

"Ronel, your chef has outdone himself!" Christian said to the uniformed waiter.

"I'm glad you enjoyed your shellfish dish, Mr. Grégoire," the waiter replied with a broad smile.

"The Sauternes was excellent also," added Augustin, emptying his glass.

"It was one of the best bottles in our cellar, sir."

Under thick eyebrows and long eyelashes, Christian glanced once more at the label. He pursed his lips in satisfaction and a faint mustache made a line on his upper lips. There was no doubt, this wine was working wonders on his taste buds.

"It seems that the warm weather in Bordeaux last year wasn't a bad thing...," he observed.

"On the contrary," Augustin added, "I think it gave the wines a certain refined potency that makes them magnificent."

"You're right, Mr. Montrose. The 1949 *millésimes* are fruity and more balanced than those of 1945."

"Mm" … said Christian. "Excellent choice, Ronel!"

"Thank you, Mr. Grégoire… Would you like some dessert? We have a delicious mocha cake sprinkled with crushed peanuts that would round off this meal nicely!"

Ronel's insistence reminded Christian that he promised to bring his sisters some pastries from *Boulangerie Saint-Marc.*

"No, not today," replied Christian as his friend also declined the desert. "You can bring us the bill, Ronel."

"Two, please," demanded Augustin.

"Oh, no!" retorted his best friend. "I invited you; the bill is mine... And I insist... Just one, Ronel."

"Very well, Mr. Grégoire."

The gray-haired waiter walked away quickly with muted steps. It was that time of the afternoon when the restaurant staff was enjoying a deserved calm before the busy hours that would come soon and continue until dawn. Though the *Rond-Point Café Restaurant* was built at the same time than the exhibition site, Christian knew the waiter for years.

"Ronel is second to none," said Augustin. "I don't know how he figures out all these wines and the dishes that best complement them."

"He started his training at my uncle's restaurant. He has a phenomenal memory... I must say, he amazes me too," added Christian, turning his head toward the large bay window.

The street was crowded with pedestrians. Among them a few workers were either going home or going to start their shifts; and tired farmers were finally arriving in town with their donkeys laden with their harvests. Several groups of tourists were also visible, hint that a cruise ship had just dropped anchor at *Quai Colomb* wharf. This was the case almost every day, boats and yachts from everywhere constantly docked in the bay of the city. Additionally, visitors being brought in by KLM and PANAM airlines were landing daily at *Chancerelles International Airport*.

"Looks like your father's negotiations went well," Christian said to his friend.

"Yes. All the travel agencies he met in Miami last year responded. There are over six million tourists coming to spend the winter there! Six million potential visitors for us!"

"Wow!" Christian marveled.

"With Haiti being highlighted in American newspapers, people will discover that we're only a couple hours away. And when they come, they'll see with their own eyes the charm of our nature and experiment the extraordinary taste of our unique rhum..."

"Without a doubt."

"The other day," Augustin continued, "my father's cousin who was visiting Lebanon told us that while he was in a movie theater in Tripoli, between showings, he saw on the screen an advertisement for the International Exhibition..."

Christian was listening with half an ear; his attention was drawn by a few tourists crossing the street. Some with cameras around their necks, others carrying burlap bags filled with souvenirs. Though happy, the small group seemed tired.

"I bet," he said, "that many travelers will visit the dance marathon."

"Certainly," Augustin added. "Tourists are everywhere now and participating in even the most unusual activities! At the travel agency, they often ask for vacation packages for islands like Ile de la Tortue! Can you imagine?!"

"No kidding," Christian laughed. "Let's hope all these advertisements won't choke us. Soon, our residential neighborhoods will be the ones seeing this influx of people when we need some quiet time to rest..."

"You're right. Vacation rentals and hotels are popping everywhere!"

Christian finished his glass of wine while following with his eyes the same group of tourists who were now entering the restaurant. Driven by curiosity, Augustin turned to see what was intriguing his friend so much.

Visibly, the tourists needed a break. Almost all of them were so pale that the little sun that looked down on them during their walk irritated their skin. The oldest one among them was particularly affected. So, the group entered lazily and happily. The owner greeted a woman in her fifties who was leading them and pointed empty tables to the exhausted tourists.

Dressed in a pale blue dress, the fifty-year-old woman's curly hair was gathered in a bun under a round hat. She delicately wiped her face while talking with the dining room manager. Her back turning to them, Christian and Augustin could not hear what she was saying. She was speaking calmly in a tone that was not disturbing the rest of the clients despite the slight commotion her group's arrival created in the restaurant. From the way the manager smiled at her and the way the waiters were following her orders, all could understand that she was a regular.

"Is that Mrs. Volmar?" asked Christian.

"Yes... it seems so," agreed Augustin.

Christian was right. The woman in blue was indeed Lynn Volmar, a childhood friend of his mother. They both had German fathers who immigrated to Haiti at the end of the 19th century. Although they shared the same roots, Lynn Volmar was the antithesis of Elsa Grégoire. Mrs. Volmar was not one of those housewives who tended her flower gardens and repeatedly threw receptions to find a suitable match for her daughters. Rather, she was one of those who was always pushing for the liberation of the mind. She was the one working on shaping Port-au-Prince cultural life.

"That woman is unbelievable!" exclaimed Christian. "She never rests!"

"All entertainment and activities held at the *Bord-de-Mer* are approved through her office," Augustin informed.

"Really? Then the dancing marathon will be magnificent."

"Who you're telling? She's a very sophisticated woman."

"With her feet firmly on the ground, though," added Christian. "That's what I like about her."

"That must be why the competitions are held at the *Cité de l'Exposition* (Expo City) and not in one of those uptown clubs."

From their table, Christian and Augustin discreetly greeted Lynn Volmar as she finally noticed them. She immediately apologized in German to the vacationers and walked purposefully toward the two young men.

"Mrs. Volmar!" said Christian, getting up from his chair. "You'll excuse us for taking so long to recognize you. Your hat is magnificent."

"How kind of you..."

The two young men exchanged the customary affectionate *bisous* with Mrs. Volmar.

"I'm so glad to see you," said Mrs. Volmar while handing Christian an envelope and a magazine from her bag. "This will save me a trip to your house. The Vogue magazine is for your sisters. There's an exceptional article about Haiti inside. As for the envelope, please give it to your parents. It's the invitation to the inauguration of the *Musée du Peuple Haïtien* (Museum of the Haitian People) next week."

"Just last night, my parents were talking about that. They thought you have forgotten them."

"Not at all. I'm very busy these days at the *Secrétairerie d'État au Tourisme* (Ministry of Tourism). I'm planning the visit of Daniel Santos."

"Really?!" said Augustin who was a fan of the Puerto Rican singer.

"Yes. He'll be here for a while. It's his first visit, and we want it to be unforgettable."

"He has become a true ambassador of the Haitian culture," said Augustin.

"Yes, indeed. So much that he intends to host and broadcast radio programs about our country in other countries of the Caribbean and Latin America."

"Wow... And where will he perform?"

"Mainly at the Simbie Night Club."

"Ah! That's where the 100 Hours dance marathon will be held," said Christian.

"Exactly," agreed Mrs. Volmar. "I wanted him to be the host, but he's scheduled to leave before the competition begins."

Mrs. Volmar turned toward the tourists she was leading. The group was laughing, being amused by the restaurant owner. With his usual humor, he was recommending the best Creole dishes on his menu.

"You are excellent dancers," said Mrs. Volmar. "You should both participate in this contest."

The remark made the young men smile. They were indeed dance enthusiasts, and all of Port-au-Prince knew it. No music seemed to hold any secrets for them. They knew how to lead their partners from a waltz to the rhythmic steps of a salsa, a *méringue*, a bolero, or a tango.

"That's our intention," replied Christian.

"We already danced 10 hours straight once," informed Augustin.

"We're up for the 100-hour challenge!"

"It will indeed be a challenge," confirmed Lynn Volmar. "But I'm sure you'll win."

Ronel brought the bill over just as Mrs. Volmar was returning to her table and tourists. Christian looked at it, then took a few bills out of his leather wallet, put them inside the book, and left a tip for the waiter under his wine glass.

The intimate atmosphere of the restaurant was insulated from the bustling street outside. American cars were lining up everywhere even in areas that were still in construction. A few pavilions were not yet ready for the official inauguration, which was fast approaching. Architects, artisans, and artists could still be seen everywhere. Pedestrians going about their business were rapidly passing the slow-pacing tourists, whom, with their cameras, were capturing any and everything: the perfect layout of the streets, a curious child peering at them, or simply lush gardens.

The Cadillac Coup Deville series 62 of Christian's father was parked in front of the restaurant; its black-ink body absorbed the afternoon sun. It was gleaming with its front chrome and metallic roof. The original advertisement from Cadillac stated that it was "a smart new Cadillac body type, designed for those who seek the low-swept lines and open-airiness of a convertible – combined with the comfort, convenience and safety of a closed car."

That unique family car was Mr. Grégoire's pride and joy. He was planning on showing it off a few weeks later at a luxury car competition. It's only under very specific circumstances that he agreed to share it with his son. But Christian knew that it was an excuse for his father to take a break from the obligations of chauffeuring the ladies of the house. Therefore, Christian took great pleasure in enjoying the paternal jewel; from time to time, he willingly agreed to be the chauffeur and the designated chaperone for Marie-Agnès, his older sister, Marie-Cécile, his youngest, and also his mother.

"Do you remember where the registration for the contest will be held?" asked Augustin.

"No," replied Christian, unbuttoning his cream-colored jacket. "But it's in the newspaper. There's a small bookstore right near the bakery; we'll stop there and buy a copy."

Christian started the engine and slid into the line of cars circulating at the roundabout before taking the direction of *Grand-Rue* Street. The boulevard, like many streets in downtown, was where one could find the best fabric shops, the best tailors, and an incredible choice of grocery stores and bakeries.

Boulangerie Saint-Marc also overlooked this bustling avenue. Christian and Augustin enjoyed the offerings of this favorite bakery. Although spacious, it was always full; the daily smells of hot bread were attracting customers like a magnet.

Behind a large and long counter, workers were busy fulfilling the orders of pressing patrons.

"Look at these cornstarch cookies," said Augustin. "We'll need several of these melting little pastries to give us strength during the marathon."

"And these *langues de bœuf* (sweet flaky pastries) won't hurt either," replied Christian. "The light sugar coating on top will be enough to boost up our determination."

Christian and Augustin each ordered bread and a few pastries before leaving the bakery.

"The bookstore is over there," said Christian, who could no longer resist the urge to bite into a cornstarch cookie.

"I can't wait to see the list of competitors," said Augustin before taking a big bite on a cookie his friend gave him. "Rumor has it that all the young ones in Port-au-Prince want to participate."

"They can't compete with us. You'll see, we will just make a little effort and they will all give up!" said Christian in a burst of laughter.

The door of the small bookstore, specializing in Haitian literature, was wide open. A few locals and foreigners were leafing through books and magazines. Augustin greeted everyone who crossed his path by tipping his hat. He headed straight for the latest poetry collections, while Christian was going to the newsstand. Christian picked up the newspaper and joined Augustin, who was reading an excerpt from a poem.

"It's fascinating. The entire collection is written in Creole."

"Who's the author?" asked Christian.

"I don't know him. But I'm going to buy it. I've always wanted to learn to read Creole... They say it's very easy. You read it as it's written."

"Hmm," said Christian, sounding disinterested.

Once back into the car, Christian frantically searched for the marathon advertisement page.

"Here!" he said in a fleeting moment. "GRAND CHAMPIONNAT DE DANSE DE RESISTANCE. The dance competition is in a week. We already have Mireille, Agathe, and Jocelyn as partners. They're all strong women. Besides, they are all part of a folk group..."

"Good, because these 100 hours of dancing will be a real test of endurance. It won't be a joke."

"The ideal thing would be for each of us to have two partners, but I can't seem to find a fourth girl," admitted Christian.

"It's not easy to meet girls who want to take on such a challenge," Augustin acknowledged. "Too bad my sister isn't here anymore..."

"Oh yeah... Did your mother and her arrive in Belgium safely?"

"Yes. My sister is starting boarding school this Monday."

Augustin was mentally searching for a girl within their circle. Who would want to dance for 100 hours? Who, without pretending a migraine, would stand on their hurting feet and not give up after a few hours?

"And yet, finding a partner shouldn't be so difficult," Augustin reflected. "5,000 *gourdes* ($1,000 USD) is a considerable amount of money for many, especially now after the government's attempt to raise the minimum wage to 3 *gourdes* ($0.60 USD) failed abruptly."

"Exactly..."

Augustin's heart jumped suddenly. He thought of a girl, one who would make him happy, if she agreed.

"Do you think Marie-Agnès will want to be my partner?"

Christian's eyes widened in astonishment. Was Augustin delirious or what? Was he talking about the Marie-Agnès, his sister, with the long, delicate fingers; the one who smiled but never laughed out loud; the one who spoke in a soft, calm voice; and that one would dance for four days and four nights under the gaze of a crowd of strangers? Christian shook his head with a mocking half-smile, amused by the thought.

"You're kidding, right?!" he let slip.

It's been a while since Christian was trying to understand why his friend was so in love with his sister. Was it because he, for his part, had never experienced such amorous feelings? Both returned from Switzerland just after the war, with their accounting degrees. Both were working in a prosperous sisal export company. Both would soon take over the businesses their respective parents would leave them. Christian will inherit the Guest House that his father had just acquired jointly with Augustin's father, and Augustin, the travel agency. Being tall, slim, and of a griffe complexion, Augustin had an incredible choice among all these women who were less formal than Marie-Agnès and who, at social gatherings, had eyes only for him.

Christian patted his friend's shoulder, feeling sorry for him.

"Man, Marie-Agnès is interested in nothing but music. Stop thinking about her, would you?"

Augustin felt hurt. Why should she stop being 'his everything'? Was he not intelligent, handsome or rich enough to be Marie-Agnès's fiancé? Or was it his low degree of European lineage that made him ineligible to reach the woman of his dreams? The young man gritted his teeth, annoyed and saddened at being rejected based on pedigree.

A brief silence fell. The Cadillac was arriving at the *Champ de Mars* district, in front of the *Hôtel Excelsior.* A small crowd was already there lining up for the dance marathon's registration.

"By the way… I didn't want to tell you," Christian said as he parked the car, "but right after her concert at the *Rex Théâtre,* my sister will be leaving for Austria on a scholarship."

Augustin's face froze in shock.

"What?! For how long?!"

"I don't know. For the duration of her scholarship, I suppose."

Augustin suddenly felt devastated; those years spent in Switzerland far from Marie-Agnès weighed on his mind. He felt the pain that consumed him while he was away from her. A photo of the small group of friends taken during their teenage years was then his only consolation; the young lady's restrained smile, her oval face, her almond-shaped eyes, her entire appearance were seared in his mind. After his studies, how many opportunities had he turned down because of her! He wanted to be in her presence constantly, to be near her; to share her joys, share her successes... And now, just when he thought he had a chance, she was leaving!

Augustin closed the newspaper on his lap. He knew the young lady's passion for the piano. He knew that more than anything else in the world, becoming a concert pianist was what she cherished the most in life; if not that, then, at the very least, a music teacher. But perhaps he was the one who had chosen the wrong career. Perhaps he should have inserted himself in her own world, more versed in classical music she mastered.

That news robbed Augustin of all hope. He seemed unable to seduce Marie-Agnès while they were living near each other, in the same city. What was he going to do if she was far, very far away?

Augustin took a deep breath. He could not let himself be defeated like this! He was going to break his silence, gather his courage, be clear and direct...

"Don't drop me off at home," he said. "Your mother promised a rose graft to mine. I'll go pick it up."

"I thought our gardener was going to plant it when your mother got back?"

"Why wait for her to come back? It'll be a surprise..."

Christian smiled and understood the excuse Augustin just concocted to accompany him to his house.

The sun was setting when they finally reached the Bois-Verna neighborhood. The streets were deserted. The quiet and calm enhanced the majesty of the neighborhood. The full beauty of the cluster of Gingerbread houses was hidden by low walls adorned with lushed tall bougainvillea shrubs. Beautiful gardens encircled all styles of these highly embellished homes.

Christian and Augustin knew the area very well. Born a few months apart, they were inseparable from the start. They grew up exploring the upper-class neighborhood. As kids, they rallied other young ones around them and formed clubs where they exchanged avant-garde ideas and dreams…

After passing Augustin's house, one street further down, Christian went through his house's wrought iron gate. He drove around the fountain that stood in the middle of the courtyard and parked the car in front of the central entrance. The mild January climate was bringing out the beauty of Mrs. Grégoire's roses collection.

"I think it's this orange color your mother wanted..."

"I think so..."

Augustin was speaking mechanically, listening to a repetitive sound of a *méringue* filling the silence. This way of repeating the musical line hinted at the fact that Marie-Agnès was at the piano.

"She's here!" Augustin said to himself, his heart pounding.

The friends started to climb a few steps when Christian felt his jacket pocket with a worried expression.

"I forgot the invitation and the magazine. I'll be right back."

While Christian was returning to the car, Augustin let himself to the large porch that wrap around the Grégoire's house. He stopped in front the living room's French door and opened it slightly. He saw first Miss Dreyfus, the piano teacher. He was well acquainted with her. His own father introduced her to the Grégoire family years before. Miss

Dreyfus was then fleeing the ravages of World War II which decimated Greece, her native land. Possessing a deep sense of freedom, her choice of refuge went to Haiti, a land that she knew extended first a hand in recognizing the independence of her country in 1822 from the Ottoman Empire. She arrived on Haitian soil a few years ago and was charmed by the Caribbean hospitality. She settled down and immediately offered the best she had: the love of the piano.

Miss Dreyfus stood rigidly in a dark dress; her silky blond hair was pulled back; and her light grayish eyes were shining as she passionately instructed her student in perfect French.

"I must feel the movement. The audience must see the mountains, the wildflowers, the birds! They must smell the fresh air. You must bring to life this *Chant de la Montagne* as if Justin Elie himself was writing it before our eyes. Come on! A little more movement this time, please!"

Marie-Agnès, a young woman twenty-five years of age, resumed her movements without batting an eye. Since she began learning the piano as a child, Augustin had not once seen her complain or look for an excuse to evade her practice sessions. Every day, she would go through her scales before moving on to studying various pieces by virtuosos.

Augustin's heart rate quickened, moved once again by this constant quest for perfection. How he would give his life to prove to her that he could be the one to support her in her passion for music! Augustin would have stood there all afternoon, watching Marie-Agnès's every move, if it hadn't been for Christian tugging at his arm.

A few laughs guided them to the rest of the family sitting at the other end of the porch.

"Christian! Augustin!" Marie-Cécile called out when she saw them.

"Good evening, everyone!" her brother said, handing her the bag of pastries and the latest Vogue issue.

Augustin greeted first the ladies before shaking Mr. Grégoire's hands. The latter was sipping a tart cherry juice freshly made from the cherry trees in the garden.

"I thought that you would return early to go shopping with your sisters for the recital at the *Rex Théâtre,*" Roger Grégoire asked his son.

The smile on Augustin's lips disappeared, saddened to have missed this golden opportunity to spend some time alone with Marie-Agnès.

"Good God!" exclaimed Christian while placing his hat and newspaper on a small table. "I completely forgot. We can go now if you like..."

"No problem. Gisèle and Violette stopped by and we went out with Mr. Volmar. I am so glad, because there was only one bottle left of the perfume I wanted," replied Marie-Cécile, munching on a *tablèt pistach* (peanut candy).

"Actually, I just saw Mrs. Volmar at the *Rond-Point*."

Christian took his parents' invitation out of the lining of his jacket.

"Finally!" exclaimed Mr. Grégoire.

"And where have you been all day?" Elsa Grégoire asked her son.

"Running Dad's errand. Then Augustin and I signed up for the 100 Hours dance."

"What's that?" asked Marie-Cécile.

"A competition where the dancer, who completes 100 hours or something like that, will win $1,000 USD or 5,000 *gourdes*," explained Christian. "It's been all over the newspapers for over a month now."

"Wow," marveled Marie-Cécile. "And who are you going to dance with?"

"Professional dancers who perform quite often at the *Théâtre de Verdure* and all over the country..."

"Yet," Augustin added, "we'll be missing a partner."

Marie-Cécile's became goggle-eyed.

"I would love to participate," she said enthusiastically.

Mrs. Grégoire looked sternly at her daughter, who immediately felt silent. She understood that her mother had no intention of considering the idea. Marie-Cécile grimaced.

"Unbelievable! So, we're copying everything!" her father exclaimed.

"Exactly," Mrs. Grégoire approved with a grim expression. "We're losing our values and adopting those of others..."

"But what are you talking about?" Christian asked, looking puzzled.

"Marathon dances aren't new, my son," Mr. Grégoire said. "They were already occurring when I was your age. This trend came from North America in the 1930s. These dances could last for days, if not months."

Christian and Augustin smiled. They were very fond of dancing but not to the point of doing it for a whole month.

"It's not a joke," continued Mr. Grégoire. "Under the weight of fatigue, the partners clung to each other or slept on each other's shoulders to keep from collapsing!"

"Wasn't this the same kind of marathons that took place in France in 1932 in the city of Orleans?" asked Mrs. Grégoire. "The brother of a friend almost died of a heart attack while participating!"

"Precisely," confirmed her husband. "And it wasn't just fatigue that was the cause, but also despair..."

"My God!" exclaimed Marie-Cécile, disgusted.

Christian bowed his head, amused by his parents' and sister's reaction.

"Actually," continued his father in complete seriousness, "it started in the States during the Great Depression that followed the first financial crisis in 1920 and then the Wall Street Crash of 1929. It was an unparallel economic disaster. Those who participated in these walkathons, as they were called, did so in a context of profound crises that plunged entire families into famine and poverty."

"We can understand why they needed the money then," Augustin acknowledged.

"Yes, and the food they served there too. Because meals were guaranteed for all those who hold on in the competition. And I'm talking about breakfast, lunch, and dinner."

"Anyway," said Christian, "we're not doing this for the money or the food. We just want to take on a challenge."

"What challenge?" asked Marie-Cécile, perplexed.

"Dancing for four days without stopping!"

Mrs. Grégoire grew despondent by the response.

"But what self-respected young woman would agree to stay for four days so close to a man who isn't her husband? This is unbelievable! These are things we would never have seen or even heard of just a few years ago! Good God, where is the world going?!" Mrs. Grégoire exclaimed.

"Hm...The Second War left real scars on our society!" Mr. Grégoire added.

Mrs. Grégoire sat stiffly in her *dodine* (rocking chair). Her subtle makeup enhanced her complexion, which, like her husband's, was neither too light nor too dark. Her lipstick was beautifully applied on her full lips; traits she passed on to her daughters. She almost closed her eyes as she looked at her son and his friend with a stern expression.

In a city like Port-au-Prince, where everyone knew each other, her son's participation in such a walkathon would not remain a secret. If the slightest rumors could easily appear in the tabloids, no need to talk about if the full story could be verified by the gossiping eyes of the curious!

Elsa Grégoire felt a light headache. She, coming from a line of bankers and who is happily married to an influential man at the Department of Finance, how could she allow her son to take part in such a thing? Mrs. Grégoire sensed disaster, already seeing her family being ridiculed, and their reputation dragged through the mud on the radio and in the country's daily newspapers.

"So," she blurted out, "among all the wonderful activities taking place at the *Bord-de-Mer*, is it to this degrading affair you signed up for?"

"Degrading?" Christian retorted. "Mother, what's so degrading about dancing?"

"Don't you understand? It's not just about dancing, it's about debauchery! You're neither engaged to nor you're a family member of these young women. Do you want people to speak badly about our families?"

Augustin turned pale. He had never seen his participation in that light. He did not know the history of dance marathons and destroying his parents' reputation was certainly the last thing he wanted to do. The young man was suddenly afraid. His participation visibly was exasperating Marie-Agnès's parents. This is not what he wanted to happen at such a crucial moment. He has not started his romantic pursuit yet.

Mrs. Grégoire's remark also made her husband pensive. Roger Grégoire nodded his head while smoothing his graying mustache. His wife was right. At the Department of Finance, he was the one who signed the state employee checks. He had a fine and unshaken reputation. A few months ago, because he was also a polyglot, he was chosen by the Central Bank to represent the country at a conference held in Spain. However, his position was not given without merit. Before him, his own father had never been able to advance beyond the position of teller. He studied hard and he married well. He had the fortune to meet Elsa, a young Jäger girl, whose German father had great connections. Through his acquaintances he was able to advance meteorically in the financial sector... At almost sixty years old, after so many years of hard and exemplary work, could he really allow his surname to be mentioned in a walkathon?

"Mother," fought back Christian, "if our registration makes people talk badly about our families, then it's the reputation of almost every family in the country that will be ruined."

Christian picked up the newspaper he had left on the table and opened it as he continued, searching for a particular page.

"Because, in today's newspaper, there are surnames in no need of money who have decided to participate."

"And who, for example?" his mother asked calmly.

"Franco Francini."

Mrs. Grégoire almost choked on a sip of cherry juice. Could this be the same Francini she had been trying to invite for so many months now, the best suitor for Marie-Agnès? The same Francini whose Italian parents opened a boutique of fine European wines downtown?

"Ah!" her son said, clearly seeing her astonishment. "There's also Georges Alphone, Max Belmont... See for yourself."

"Alphone?" asked Mr. Grégoire. "The grandson of the former Haitian ambassador?"

"In the flesh," confirmed Christian. "And Max Belmont, the son of the owner of the cargo ship Belmont Terminals Limited."

Mrs. Grégoire was speechless, stunned by so many "good families" who had agreed to let their children participate in such a competition.

"The newspaper, please," demanded Mr. Grégoire who wanted to see the partial list of the participants with his own eyes.

"Several local retailers will sponsor the event," said Christian. "Bulova Watches, Hayti Trading Co., Goodyear Tires, Chevrolet dealership, Bata Shoes, Frank Wilson, Nazon Distillery, the National Ice Factory... They will all sponsor an hour a day on the radio!"

Marie-Cécile stared at her parents. She didn't understand their confused stern expression compare to the enthusiasm of her brother she so much admired.

"Is this competition really that bad?" she asked.

"Not at all," replied her brother. "It's like when we go to *Cabane Choucoune* on Saturday nights, nothing more, nothing less. They say it will be unique, sensational, extraordinary, incredible, but true!"

Ms. Grégoire began to laugh, amused by the comparison between a club as exclusive as *Cabane Choucoune* in the hills of Pétion-Ville and a nightclub where popular singers and dancers were mingling in the sketchiest part of town.

Mrs. Grégoire let out a deep sigh, feeling that it was time for her to get involved in her son's life. The time had come now to quickly find a suitable match to help him settling down. This would then put an end to his comings and goings with Augustin and prevent her son from debasing the family's name throughout the country.

Elsa Grégoire straightened up first and looked Christian straight in the eyes.

"We are the Jägers and the Grégoires. Illustrious families made up of respectable and dignified citizens for generations. There is no way any of my children, any of you, will participate in this cheap marathon. Am I understood?" she said emphasizing each syllable of the question.

Christian replied nothing. He simply stared at the floor. Augustin was deeply bothered by the scene before him. A frozen smile on his lips, he looked at Marie-Cécile, who was furtively glancing at her parents' glacial faces.

The falling silence was greatly amplified by the sound of the piano coming from the living room. Augustin felt an enormous pressure on his spine. He knew that he would not be able to talk to Marie-Agnès that day. So, he stood up slowly, ready to take his leave.

Christian took his friend's departure as an excuse to escape his mother's fury.

"I don't know what we should do…" Augustin said as he walked toward the entrance gate.

"Don't worry," Christian reassured. "By the time she thinks about the names of all the families who will be participating, she'll change her mind."

"Well, I have to talk to my father about it also," Augustin said as he stepped out into the street. "It's not a done deal for me either. In any case, even if he agrees, without you, I won't participate."

Augustin left his friend and walked slowly home with a frown on his face, his hands in his pockets. Marie-Agnès was leaving soon for Austria. He must not hold back any more. It was time to act, get closer to her, show her his overflowing love. He needed to sear in her mind pleasant images of him; he was fully aware she will find herself surrounded by suitors in that distant and who will admire undoubtedly her beauty, her refinement, her education, and her incomparable talent. This was not the time to meddle in social perceptions and disagreements.

Augustin felt like screaming with rage. He had to find a solution as quickly as possible.

CHAPTER 3
The Visionary of *Portail St. Joseph*

Miles away from the Grégoires' residence, the teeming commercial district of Portail Saint-Joseph was in full swing that afternoon. A real bazaar of fruits, vegetables, food supplies, fabrics, hats, and various goods were spread out on the ground or makeshift tables at the *Gare du Nord* famers' market. The horns of pickup trucks and some private car echoed, competing with the incessant haggling between sellers and buyers looking for bargains on items left over from the day.

This chaotic mercantile activity, however, did not prevent the more established boutiques, grocery stores, import and export companies located in various neighboring streets to conduct business as usual. Most had been there for a short time, while others had, against all odds, overcome all the setbacks of the Haitian economy. The latter ones were housed in old 19th century buildings. *Au Petit Dindon*, owned by the Cantave family, was one of them in this Portail Saint-Joseph commercial district.

The clock just struck four that afternoon, as twenty-year-old Emilio Cantave standing behind the counter, was helping his mother count the proceeds of the day. The worn *gourde* bills, imbued with various scents, bore the imprint of the daily struggles of those who had handled them. Methodically, *Madan* Vic (Mrs Vic), a forty-five-year-old woman, owner and manager of the business, slipped them in the bottom of her completely worn leather purse.

The repetitive metal sounds of hundreds of coins broke the silence as Emilio recorded the earnings in a student notebook. He took his time dividing the sheets, labeling each column with quantities, expenditures, receipts, deficits, and profits. His entries were like calligraphy; a style he carefully honed anticipating the moment he would finally realize his dream of becoming a certified public accountant.

"Aren't you rehearsing today?" his mother suddenly asked him.

"Yes, as soon as I get home," replied the young man.

The rehearsal of which *Madan* Vic was talking about consisted of weight training sessions, exercises, and dance routines that the young man and his twin sister, Marie Emilia, were practicing. They were also concocting strategies that would help them win the dance marathon.

"The day is getting near. You need to build up muscles. You both need to eat some more liver, banana, watercress, and polenta with spinach and herring. This will strengthen you... You both must make your father proud."

For a moment, the memory of his father brought sadness to Emilio's eyes. Then, just as quickly, his features relaxed and he smiled affectionately at his mother.

"Don't worry... I promise: your sacrifices won't be in vain."

"You'd better," his mother told him, staring at him with her hazel eyes.

Emilio stopped writing and put his arm around *Madan* Vic's shoulders.

"I'm the one who balance every day," he said tenderly. "I know how much we need those 5,000 *gourdes* to expand the store and pay off debts, plus the costs of Dad's accident."

Madan Vic bowed her head slightly, holding back tears. Just a few months ago, she almost lost her husband before her eyes. Lucien Victorin Cantave suffered a heart attack. From a stepladder, he fell in the middle of the store while reaching for a can of food. He broke a leg and two ribs. *Madan* Vic screamed in horror at the sight of the mingled body of her husband. A few customers and other neighborhood merchants rushed over upon hearing the horrible screams. All wanted to help their Vic, the kind-hearted merchant.

That day, everything could have quickly spiraled into irreparable disaster for the family. But Emilio, understanding the duty thrusted upon him to take care of his five brothers and sisters, did not hesitated to assume the position of the elder son. He quitted his job at a furniture workshop specializing in products out of mahogany and become his mother's right-hand man and the moral support the entire family needed.

From the very beginning, the visionary mind of Emilio which he inherited from his father, came alive. From a second-hand bookseller, he acquired an accounting manual, spent nights reading, and referring to it repeatedly when necessary. He applied the principles he could understand in the grocery store. Then, he introduced some much-needed innovations to the business and worked seven days a week to boost revenue.

"Before," *Madan* Vic recalled, "your father was a good dancer. We met at a summer ball. He was so handsome…"

The distant look in *Madan* Vic eyes revealed the depth of her love for her husband but also all the pain she felt then.

"I know, *Manman* (Mom)...He never stopped repeating you're the most beautiful of all women..."

"Anyway..." replied *Madan* Vic simply in a low voice tone with a discreet smile on her lips.

Emilio's mother took another bag and placed a tray of stale bread inside. Emilio began inspecting the grocery store after finishing his counting task. Everything was in order. The freshest breads were in their display cases. On the shelves, cans of sardines lined up side by side, their labels clearly visible. Even though their aroma was filling the space, the crates of salted fish, so beloved by the customers, were hermetically sealed. Cups, tin items, and tin-glazed ceramic utensils hung in clusters from the ceiling. The soaps, that Marguerite, two years Emilio's senior, had made herself, were displayed in a pyramidal shape which attracted attention and desire. The floor was well polished. The two high straw chairs on which they sat to rest when there were no customers, were overturned on top of each other.

Holding a set of heavy keys, Emilio followed his mother out of the building. He locked the double wooden doors behind them. Noticing his mother's slow steps and her hunched back, Emilio picked up one of the bags she was carrying and set off toward their home in the lower *Lalue* neighborhood. Passing before a row of shops, *Madan* Vic greeted a few other retailers who were still busying themselves at various things at this late hour.

"I need to see a friend in the neighborhood of Bel Air," *Madan* Vic said with heavy eyes. "She makes beautiful straw handbags that we could sell."

"You've done too much today, *Manman*. If rehearsal ends early, I'll go see her in your place," the young man objected in a worried voice.

"No. Monday will be better. Marguerite will be with us working in the store; so around noon, you'll go see what my friend has. Your idea from the other day was good: we need more diversity. But today, focus on the competition. It's more important."

If the matriarch, Marthe Cantave, inherited her father's hazel eyes and her *grimèl* complexion (light-skin complexion), she was not born into luxury and money. Marthe's father was a Lebanese immigrant who arrived in Haiti alone and broke at the end of the 19th century. He settled in the city of Gonaïves. After a while, he started to sell all the items he could carried with him on the streets. This attracted the disdain of the locals. When he died at a very old age, he left little to his children, except resilience and the will to succeed. By marrying Lucien Victorin

Cantave, Marthe abandoned her status of daughter of an immigrant and became *Madan* Vic (Mrs Vic). She became a woman who would devote all her energy to making her husband's dreams come true while also working hard to build her children's future.

"It's a shame we no longer have our aluminum cast business," she lamented. "We would have sold a lot of them."

"The competition in that business was too fierce, *Manman*. What we're doing now is a business of a higher class."

The word "class" struck *Madan* Vic with a resounding shock. She, the daughter of an immigrant who had suffered the consequences of her father's misfortunes throughout her childhood and who, out of nothing, started a grocery business with her husband, felt her son's remark as an insult. *Madan* Vic stopped walking, gripping Emilio firmly by the arm.

"Listen to me carefully: It's not class that allows your father and me to feed and send you all to school. It's this!" she said, repeatedly pointing to her brain with her index finger. "Even though I can't read or write, it's thanks to this that your father and me were able to survive during the war!"

Emilio turned his head away as his mother resumed her steps. He hated that severe look he knew too well. He felt deep within him the pressure of his mother's hand on his arm. Emilio remembered the relentless lessons his parents taught them; he remembered the hard-work ideal that was instilled in them, their thirst for success. He understood all of that very clearly and not once had he trivialized their many sacrifices. But this speech was too much.

"Mom, sorry if you misunderstood my words," he apologized. "What I mean is that we need to diversify. There are many tourists visiting the country now. They can't take a kettle with them as a souvenir. But Marguerite's soap and embroidered items, your friend's handbags, could serve as wonderful gifts. And every tourist who leaves with one of our items will be advertising our business all over the world... Look! Alfred is learning well the wood polishing technics that I'm teaching him. He can make bowls and small sculptures from mahogany wood. And when the business grows even bigger, Béatrice can join me in doing counts."

Madan Vic did not reply. She was thinking. Béatrice, one of her daughters, aged twenty-two, was the only one who, after receiving her *brevet* (middle school diploma) decided to become a typist and stenographer. She seemed completely disinterested in the family's business, constantly striving to imitate her favorite movie actresses. If *Au Petit Dindon* became a successfully grocery business, perhaps she could be enticed to join the family business; perhaps, she could see that it is in her best interest.

As for Liliane, who was only fifteen and would soon receive her own *brevet,* she would provide the help that Emilia, Marguerite, and herself needed. With her culinary skills, she and Emilia could make additional pastries to supplement the *dous makos* (sweets made from sweetened condensed milk, flavored with vanilla) that Victorin's aunt was sending them from her hometown of *Petit-Gonâve.*

Alfred, eighteen-years old, would leave his part-time job at the dry cleaning to begin his apprenticeship in carpentry. In addition to mastering the making of small collectibles and in increasing his skills, he could easily become a cabinetmaker. He could use the courtyard at the back of the store for the furniture orders that were sure to arrive.

Madan Vic approved. Emilio was not entirely wrong.

"God willing, one day *Au Petit Dindon* will be a big business," she said with conviction.

Emilio nodded silently. But deep down, he knew that this dream would never see the light of day if they did not quickly pay off their debts. He needed to put his energy into earning the 5,000 *gourdes.*

Marthe Cantave continued the conversation, but Emilio was barely listening. He was just thinking about the dance steps he was going to try with his sister. They were some tricks his father taught him that morning and he was impatient to put them into practice.

As they walked toward the neighborhood of Lalue, the usual commotion of Portail Saint-Joseph dissipated. The fresh air of the late afternoon drew occupants of houses onto their small porches to greet passersby or to share the latest news in the neighborhood. Emilio and his mother stopped in front of the porch of a *komè* (gossipy female friend) whose baby was teething.

"How's the little one?" asked *Madan* Vic. "Has the fever gone?"

"Yes, neighbor," replied the young mother wearily. "Thanks for the tea."

"Anytime... I've been through this six times, and I haven't lost one," said *Madan* Vic, proudly patting Emilio's shoulder. "Don't worry. And if you need more tea, don't hesitate to come and pick some leaves in the yard."

Madan Vic touched her neighbor's hand to comfort her before continuing her way.

The southern part of the Lalue neighborhood was a cluster of stylish wooden houses, built on concrete bases, attached to one another. It's been only three years since Emilio was living with his family in this neighborhood, which gradually was becoming a part of the middle class. His father, who was always scrutinizing reforms, discerned one day that something would change their lives. Indeed, one had this effect: 'prohibition to increase rent excessively'. This law came at a time when his parents were seriously considering moving the family out of the commercial area to be closer to the intellectual elite. Like Béatrice and Liliane, Emilio loved books, and this change reawakened his long-forgotten dreams of studying.

When Emilio and his mother arrived to their Gingerbread style house, he pushed open the small entrance gate. Marguerite, twenty-four-years old, was adding the last touches to a tablecloth. The rays of the setting sun were illuminating her fingers as she was skillfully embroidering small pale pink flowers. Her father was beside her, slumped in a chair, laughing heartily at one of Alfred's jokes. The latter was talking, sitting near him and polishing his shoes. Béatrice was smiling too as she copied French lyrics from a neighbor's self-made song book. From the open living room door, Emilia waved to her mother, while she was explaining to Liliane how to store leftover food in the pantry.

Before climbing the two steps to the entrance, *Madan* Vic glanced at her potted plants that were lined up on the steps. A few dead leaves contrasted with the bright green of the ferns she was collecting. She paused for a moment to clean them; she was not going to let fatigue stop her from the meticulous work.

When Marthe Cantave finally arrived on the porch, she briefly caressed her husband head. A small smile came to her lips along with this loving gesture, a testimonial to a lifetime of struggles and complicity. She placed a kiss on her husband's receding hairline, then pulled out one of the straw chairs beside him and sat down. Fifteen years her senior, Victorin health was improving. He was looking less tired. His dark complexion was no longer grayish. He also seemed to gain muscle mass. His very dark eyes were appearing clearer.

Madan Vic took the bag of stale bread and handed it to Emilia, who was hurrying to the front door. Marie Emilia and Emilio were identical twins in many ways: they were the same average height, the same oval face and thin lips from which a broad smile often appeared. But the resemblance ended there. If the girl had her mother's very fair complexion and her paternal grandmother's extremely frizzy hair, her brother inherited Victorin's dark skin, his mother's hazel eyes and almost straight hair.

"Was it a good day at the shop, *Manman*?" asked Emilia, joining them on the porch. "Did Lobo come by asking for credit?"

All the children started laughing at the mention of the madman.

"With all the noise that guy makes," exclaimed Liliane, "his creole nickname suits him very well!"

"I have a feeling he lives somewhere inside the farmers' market," said Alfred.

"It's a good thing he didn't come today," said Emilio. "We were far too busy to pay attention to his stupid stories."

"Your mother and I have already told you all not to make fun of him," Victorin reproached his children. "What happened to him could happen to anyone. It was the loss of his children in a fire that drove him mad. When he comes by, give him something to eat or drink. That won't make us poor."

"Yes, Dad. We always do," Marguerite confirmed.

"That's my girl," *Madan* Vic congratulated. "Anyway, we had a good day, although there weren't as many customers as yesterday."

"Ross Manning Circus is back in action. Maybe they all went to see the horse show," Alfred said as he was now starting to polish Liliane's school shoes.

"Honestly, how did they train the animal to dance with such elegance?" Béatrice marveled.

"I don't understand either," said her father. "If only, in addition to waltz and tango, they also could teach them how to dance our *méringue.*"

"Ah! Ah! I'd gladly give him my place in the marathon to dance with Emilio!" Emilia exclaimed, laughing.

Since its arrival late 1949, the Ross Manning Show, with its diverse attractions, had aroused greatly the curiosity of Port-au-Prince's population. The music, the dance performances, and the array of lights and colors attracted all those starving for entertainment. The hardships of the war caused many to focus on diversions. This fair was, indeed, one of the most beautiful things that Emilio's father had ever seen. The weekend before, although he was weak, his children and wife had managed to drag him to the *Palmistes* area to relax.

"Emilio will have to borrow some strength to support

this horse for 100 hours," Liliane added cheerfully.

Liliane closed the pantry while recalling their visit. She skipped toward the gallery, the memory of the roller coaster she had ridden for the first time making her smile. She was undoing her long, wavy braids. Her jet-black hair cascaded freely over her *caïmite* complexion (reddish-brown skin color), a result of a mixing of her parents' features.

"I also liked the Ferris wheel and the carousel!"

"Yes, me too!" Béatrice interrupted cheerfully. "Do you remember our distorted silhouettes in the House of Mirrors?"

"Lord! A horror!" Marguerite blurted out, adding one last stitch to her embroidery.

When Emilio recalled the show of four men of different sizes competing for a 50-cents, they all laughed so hard they were in tears.

"Too bad you girls didn't want to see the snake act!" the young man said to his sisters.

The four sisters made a face that amused their brothers.

"On Saturday we could go to the *Théâtre de Verdure,*" suggested Alfred, running his fingers through his short, wavy black hair. "There'll be a Spanish dancers show."

"This fair will end up taking all your money," their mother pointed out.

"Anyway, I won't be able to go," said Béatrice. "The book fair at the *Maison des Écrivains* will be on that very day. Let's go after the Carnival!"

"Oh, no!" said Emilio. "I'll be in the middle of the marathon. Don't they have another date?"

"That's important!" snapped *Madan* Vic while fixing her bun with a hairpin. "The whole family has to be ready to support Emilia and you."

Béatrice rolled her hazel eyes. Although she looked exactly like her mother, with her extremely fair complexion and almost straight brown hair, only Emilio and Liliane shared her love of literature. If usually Emilio volunteered to accompany her to cultural events, this time the dance competition had the upper hand. All hope was resting on those thousands of gourdes that would change their lives.

"I can go with her," Liliane suggested.

Madan Vic stopped fixing her bun and looked at her daughter unsmilingly.

"No way that you two girls are going alone to a cultural event. Alfred won't be available, so you will have to go another time."

Béatrice blushed and felt a tinge of sadness. She had no interested in this dance marathon. She looked at her songbook with pages adorned with pictures of women in their elegant attire. She would have given anything to be in that world. As for her family's business she did not understand the allure and interest; she sincerely did not comprehend even the modus operandi: pots hung from the ceiling, fish smelling cans of food and in the middle of this mess were amazingly soaps, cheap plastic items, and embroidered tablecloths! If only her parents could understand that the future lay in travel, refinement, and luxury goods!

"I've finished my embroidery," Marguerite said to Liliane. "I can now do your hair for school tomorrow."

"How many times have I to tell you all not to do this kind of thing in the open, on the porch?!" objected *Madan* Vic. "First, there is Alfred shining shoes, and now you wanting to do Liliane's hair! Anyone can come at any times and visit us!"

"That's what I told them earlier," Victorin added slowly.

Despite his figure, Lucien Victorin Cantave was a soft man who forgave all his children's misdeeds. His wife therefore knew that he might not have spoken with them firmly. It befell on her to chastise them, to discipline them.

All the children went inside while Béatrice, following them slowly, was singing *Ma brune*, a romantic bolero. Her voice rose through the rooms with such sweetness that her parents, who remained on the front porch, began to hum along with her.

Built on a narrow lot, the single shotgun house stretched like a long corridor. The rooms flowed into one another and finally opened onto a covered porch that duplicated the dimensions of the front of the house. It was on this porch that the entire family ate their meals overlooking a well-kept backyard. *Madan* Vic and her daughters tended to a vegetable garden planted in a square spot in the backyard. Victorin was even raising a few chickens as if they were his own children.

The sun had now set and the air was becoming fresher. The neighborhood children skipped about and played in the settling calm. Marguerite lit two artisanal gas lamps as Alfred and Emilio were rearranging the space for rehearsal. In a synchronized motion, the two brothers lifted and moved around the long dining table to a corner on the porch before repositioning the chairs. Marguerite sat down and waited for Liliane who was carrying a small straw chair. Lilian sat down and abandoned her hair to the expertise of her older sister.

Béatrice was not far behind her. She had a cup of chocolate in one hand and a piece of buttered toast in the other; she sipped the drink while watching Alfred searching for a particular radio station. Once the music he wanted was found, the sound created a cheerful atmosphere that drew the rest of the family onto the porch.

The twins quickly changed into their everyday clothes; Emilia put on a skirt over a pair of trousers she borrowed from her brother. She wanted better and more freedom in her movements.

As her parents were seating down, Emilia opened a large bedsheet on the concrete floor, creating a makeshift surface for their workout. She and her brother laid down on it and faced the courtyard. They started a breathing exercise and the pure air of the evening filled their lungs creating a feeling of well-being. Then followed the relaxing breathing by an upper and lower body stretching.

“Stretch your arms well,” Victorin said commandingly. “Don't forget that the secret of resilient dancers lies in the elasticity and strength of their muscles.”

Since the day his children entered the competition, Victorin devoted time and energy in guiding them through their strengthening and flexibility exercises.

"When you're done stretching," he reminded them, "don't forget to run three laps around the yard."

Madan Vic frowned and looked at Emilia worriedly.

"Hmm," she said, "be careful with these physical exertions. They could make you barren, my child."

Emilia straightened up, increasingly annoyed by her mother's stubborn archaic thoughts.

"Mom!" she exclaimed. "My muscles need to be strong and healthy just like Emilio's. Exercises are key to good health."

"Okay!" her mother replied in a warning tone. "You have a perfect example in *Ti* Claire, our neighbor. Did you see how massive her body is? She never has been able to get married, let alone have children. All that because of these physical exercises she used to do when she was younger. They completely deformed her!"

"Her wrists are like mine. We're born with big bones. That's all."

Victorin tightened his lips. His wife's constant intervention whenever their daughter did any physical activity was also irritating him.

"Don't worry," he said. "We'll all make sure she doesn't make any abrupt movements. In the meantime, she and Emilio need to build up their endurance. Powerful muscles will help them win the competition."

Madan Vic pulled up a small straw chair to prop up her tired, heavy feet. She will never change her mind regarding exercising. She understood that a woman should stay active and not have a flabby body; but this should be for the purpose of having strong children and take care of her family. It was in no way a means to strengthen muscles to the point of transforming herself into a man.

Emilia turned her back to her mother. Her exercises targeted the shoulders, the waist, the arms, and the head. She would have liked to follow her brother's movements, but her mother was watching. She simply strengthened her arms, feet, and waist avoiding exercises *Madan* Vic would find inappropriate for a young lady.

Emilio left the mat to sit on a bench next to a number of improvised dumbbells. Alfred followed him, ready to help him lift the weights they invented using cement poured into pots of powdered milk. Victorin was happy to see his sons' ingenuity, true evidence to their determination.

Meanwhile, Emilia was moving into the courtyard with a series of small tiptoe steps followed by very short long jumps. Her supple arms rose and fell alongside her body while her feet spread gracefully like a ballerina's. Then, to strengthen her muscles, she repeatedly launched herself into the air on one leg, turning, and then landing on the other, while keeping her torso and arms wide open to follow the rotation. Getting into the excitement of her exercise, she dared to raise her knees higher.

Béatrice looked at Liliane from head to toe before focusing on the twins. Her mother's attention, her father's care for Emilio and Emilia, caused her some discomfort. A tinge of envy was buried beneath her casual demeanor.

"Left, right, left, right!" she ridiculed Emilia. "If you don't win, it certainly won't be your fault!"

Emilia glared at her sister, who laughed even harder.

"Why don't you go practice with them instead of spending your time singing or sleeping when you're not working?" Marguerite reproached.

"In case you've forgotten," Béatrice replied, wiping the corner of her lips with her index finger. "Work isn't around the corner. It's a forty-five-minute walk. And I do this every single day, rain or shine."

"But," Liliane pointed out, "we don't have a car. We all walk to get where we want to go. I also walk forty-five minutes to get to school. Four times a day, no less."

"You're young, that's normal," Béatrice retorted, looking at her nails.

Marguerite and Liliane burst out laughing, amused by the affected, ladylike air that Béatrice often mimicked. Ever since their sister acquired a book on etiquette, she no longer spoke or walked the same way. For work, Béatrice only wore suits with hats that she always tried to match with her shoes, gloves, and handbag. Their mother often complained that she barely contributed to household expenses, saving all her salary for books, clothes, and accessories that enhanced them.

Madan Vic threw her arms to the sky, which amused her other daughters even more.

"What's going on?" asked Emilia, who returned to the porch.

"Béatrice is killing us!" replied Marguerite.

Emilia and her brother sat for a moment and drank a glass of water from the large pitcher placed near the door leading into the house. Alfred returned to the radio, flipping through the stations. He finally recognized *Peze Kafe,* a popular song.

"This music is perfect!" he shouted.

All the siblings agreed. The sound of the drum pounded through the radio, rose from the porch, grew louder and louder like a call to action. Liliane was the first to stand up, to sing loudly, while Marguerite was barely completing her hairdo:

Manman m voye m peze kafe o !
Ann arivan mwen sou Pòtay la
M jwen jandam arete m!
Woy ! Sa m ap di lakay lè m a rive ?
Mezanmi ! O ! O !
Sa m ap di lakay lè m a rive !

(My mom sent me to weigh coffee!
When I arrived at the city Gate
I was arrested by the police!
God! What will I say when I get home?
Alas! Oh! Oh!
What will I say when I get home?)

Emilio pulled his sister towards him and began performing the steps he had been mulling over in his head all day. Emilia let herself be guided, completely being caught up in the lively rhythm. As her father pretended to be the drummer, her mother tapped out the rhythm with her hands.

Béatrice took the opportunity to advise Emilia on the need to be graceful in her movements, as it would set her apart from the other competitors. Alfred and Liliane agreed that the twins needed to be more energetic. Marguerite and their father, on the other hand, felt that when dancing to the rhythm, they should always remember to save their energy, as 100 hours would not pass as quickly as they might think.

CHAPTER 4
The Number

Each day that passed, the launch of the competition was nearing. Ads were repeating in a loop on several radio stations and street gossips were fueled by newspapers columns. There was a palpable expectation of the greatest event of the year and the organizers wanted everything to be spectacular.

Two meeting sessions were scheduled at the Simbie Night Club with all the future participants. On the day of the first meeting, Solon arrived sheepishly, dressed in a beige shirt and gray pants that he purchased the day before at the *odeïdes* (second-hand clothing shops). It took him a while to choose the right outfit among the racks full of foreign second-hand clothes. He did not want to arrive looking disheveled at the club.

One of the workers said that this kind of competition was for the country's *gwo zouzoun* (upper-class). And God knows that he, Solon Férila, was not of that world. His parents were small farmers whose deformed, calloused hands bore witness to years of hard work and dedication.

They were humble coffee growers who dreamed of expanding their business to join the ranks of the successful *Jérémien* traders who exported coffee to Europe. Like his parents, Solon believed too in this dream, especially when they sold their quality coffee on the local market. Solon invested his early teenage years in that vision and even more so when hurricanes repeatedly hit the region or when successive droughts seemed to mock this nourishing peninsula. How did he fail at this dream of being successful as the years flew away? How did he manage to found himself here now, among so many people from this other world?

The venue was an open-air club built on a succession of islets through which the waters of the Gulf of *La Gonâve* was meandering. Hundreds of impressive palm trees rose up everywhere on the islets, marveling the competitors. Close during the day, it was the perfect time to hold the meeting at the venue.

Rows of chairs were set up in the middle of the dance floor. The space was almost full when Solon arrived, accompanied by Shilette. He searched in vain for a familiar face, but he only encountered the eyes of curious strangers. Solon pushed out his chest, pulled up his trousers proudly, and tightened his worn belt. He adjusted the collar of his shirt, making sure it was buttoned properly. His heart was pounding. His hands were sweaty. But he absolutely did not want to show his nervousness.

Some of the competitors knew each other and huddled together, laughing nonstop. For a moment, a few of them involuntarily glanced at Solon, giving the young man the impression that they were mocking him, probably guessing at his line of work because of his burnt complexion. Solon swallowed his saliva and walked purposefully to a row where one couple was seated.

Most of the competitors were men whose postures revealed their state of mind. Some held their heads high in their tailored suits, while others displayed their insecurity with hunched backs or shifty gazes. Among these men, Solon noticed the presence of a few women. With furtive glances, he occasionally contemplated their hats elegantly perched on their heads or the suits that emphasized their slim waists. He inhaled their light perfume, which tingled his nostrils. This was far from the repulsive odors from his neighborhood. Solon could not help but admire the light reserved laughter that added a little sweetness to this adrenaline-fueled atmosphere.

However, one small group particularly caught Solon's attention. A man called Clifford F. Mayer, whom many seemed to know, was being introduced to two other competitors: one was dressed in navy blue pants and a white *guayabel* (typical south American men's shirt) and the other was in a gray striped suit.

"Mayer just came back from abroad... It wasn't long ago that he participated in a competition like this one that lasted over a month!"

The *guayabel*-wearing competitor looked at Mayer as if he stepped out from another planet.

"Well then!" he blurted out. "This marathon holds no secrets for you."

"None at all," replied the young man smugly while straightening his khaki-colored jacket.

"And," pointed out the competitor who was introducing him, "you came in third, if I'm not mistaken!"

"That's right!"

"So, there's no point in us even trying. In the first hour, you'll beat us all!" noted the other man in the striped suit.

"Every competition is different. And that's what makes it so interesting," Mayer replied proudly. "However, this one strangely reminds me of one in Paris. It was the same number of competitors, I think. But we were only men, one of whom was a solo. I came in second."

"With such a track record, they should have allowed you to compete solo. No woman will survive in your arms!" observed the competitor in *guayabel*.

The small group burst into laughter, while Solon was trembling from his chair. He glanced furtively in their direction. So, among them, there were experienced people who could prevent him from winning those 5,000 *gourdes*? If Solon would compete with his determination as his only strength, others would do so according to rules that held no secrets for them. And this Clifford F. Mayer, with his bold shoulders, his stiff head, and his gritted teeth, seemed to know them all and was already enjoying victory.

Solon's heart quickened. He thought of the sacrifices he had made; the expenses he incurred; the odd jobs he worked to get the money he needed. All these for nothing?

Solon needed reassurance. He turned and looked at Shilette. Her standing by his side calmed him down. His expression revealed all the sentiment her beauty inspired. This moon-faced girl was invoking inside of him a poetic fervor that he thought he had lost.

Even though Shilette's clothing looked less flashy than the elegant women standing in the room, her simplicity made her attractive. She wore a simple little khaki dress and a colorful headband holding back her thick hair. Even so, she did not seem at all intimidated. She had a half-smile on her lips and was looking in all directions, as if trying to spot someone. Her face was a little grayish looking, the result of her washing it with artisanal soap.

"I can't believe I'm here," she said excitedly.

"We're here to win!"

"We really need this money," Shilette said pensively.

"You're only eighteen," Solon mocked. "What are you going to do with it?"

"We want to open a restaurant in our neighborhood in *Carrefour*."

Solon gasped, surprised by the news.

"A restaurant at your place?"

"Yes, my mother wants to stop peddling on the streets."

"So, if I need to eat, I will have to go all the way to *Carrefour*? And when will your mother open this 'restaurant'?" he mocked.

Shilette shrugged her shoulders.

"I don't know," she said with a little smile, also amused by the young man's reaction.

But suddenly, Solon stopped laughing. What Shilette just revealed opened his eyes to an opportunity. With his part of the money, he could also invest in the restaurant and sell his coffee to Rosa. Through her clientele, this excellent-quality coffee could make a name for itself and gradually become famous and profitable.

As he was thinking this, Solon noticed out of the corner of his eye a man who sat just across from them. He was dressed simply like him and was alone. Amusingly, that man, from his seat, was introducing himself to anyone who paid the slight attention to him and shook their hands. It seemed as if he wanted to befriend everyone. After a while the young man's attention turned squarely on Solon and Shilette. He smiled and approached them.

"There was no need to bring your dance partner. It's just a meeting," he said.

Solon looked at the man with a surprised and confused expression. Had he met him somewhere before? Had he unknowingly shaken his hand when he arrived? If not, what was he getting involved in? What did he know about all the hassles some people went through to get here, even to get their partners? Solon smirked and made a recoiling gesture. He pressed his back against his chair and looked away.

Solon knew he would be tagged with a number as the main dancer; but he wanted Shilette to get one too. Indeed, he had to convinced Rosa to let her daughter be his partner.

His first request was met with a plethora of dismissive words that attacked his entire being. But he had a goal to achieve. So, the next day, swallowing his pride, he came back. Yet, each subsequent request and proposal clashed with Rosa's apprehensions. Her daughter was the apple of her eye. Shilette has never been anywhere with a man; she has never seriously interacted anything with any man, much less spent days in the arms of one.

However, Shilette's participation was about to open a door. For some time, Rosa felt that she no longer had the strength to keep up with her growing business. Now that the reputation of her cuisine was spreading, she needed to settle the business down somewhere. After much thought, Rosa came to realized that Solon posed no danger and that the offer came at the right time. Finally, she accepted under certain conditions.

"It will be fifty, fifty," she snapped.

"What?" Solon retorted.

"Then, go find someone else!" she returned.

Knowing Solon's awkward ways with women, Rosa confidently challenged the young man. Solon's conversations were bland, always revolving around his ability to read and write. Many times, before, Cherilus secretly asked Rosa for help in finding a companion for his friend. Therefore, convinced that her daughter was the only one Solon could find as his partner, Rosa clung to her offer.

It was hard for Solon to understand what Rosa was demanding. He was the one who came up with the idea of entering this competition; he was the one who would wear the number on his back and devote all his energy to winning the 5,000 *gourdes*. How could Rosa have dared ask for any kind of share? How could she have thought he would agree to give so much money to an eighteen-year-old girl? Solon's jaw tightened. The injustice of the request greatly irritated him.

"In your dreams!" he blurted out.

Cherilus had a hard time convincing his friend. Solon knew his worth too well. Unlike Rosa, his friend did not need anyone to read or write anything for him, much less sign his name. He may have come from the countryside, but he wasn't an illiterate country boy.

Regardless Solon needed a partner for the contest. Cherilus thought about the women he knew, but none seemed capable enough to stay a hundred hours in the race with his friend. Cherilus had to reason with him; and after several days, Solon calmed down, realizing that, after all, 2,500 *gourdes* ($500 USD) was quite a bounty. So, he surrendered to Rosa's offer…

Remembering this episode, Solon let out a small sigh and stared again at the "advisor" sitting in front of him. How cheeky! he thought. He let out a meaningful "hmm" from the back of his throat.

A couple sitting in the row was following the conversation. The young man particularly seemed amused as much by Solo's grin as by the "hmm" he let out. He had to put his hand over his mouth to suppress a laughter.

Solon noticed the reaction and looked at him. Though the young man was not exuding a countenance of superiority, everything about him was intriguing. His dark complexion was contrasted with translucent hazel eyes and straight hair.

"Emilio," said the young man, presenting himself.

"Solon."

"Is she your sister?"

"No. That's Shilette, a friend."

Shilette, who was staring at her unkempt nails, looked up and let out a muffled sound of wonderment, flashing a shy smile that accentuated her deep dimples and lit up her face.

"Ah, okay," said Emilio. "My partner is my twin sister, Marie Emilia."

Emilia leaned forward to greet Solon and Shilette. Solon bowed slightly to greet her. He noticed her much fairer complexion, her frizzy hair, and her dark eyes. He wondered, intriguingly, how, two people born on the same day, despite having similar features, could be so different. But he did not dare to ask.

"I didn't think there would be so many people," Emilio observed.

"Me neither," replied Solon, looking around the room. "A co-worker mentioned it to me, and I signed up."

"We heard it on the radio. And where do you work?"

"I'm a gardener in the *Palmistes* area."

"So, you're fully part of this experiment!"

"My mother would have adopted you in a heartbeat," offered Emilia. "She loves plants so much..."

Emilia stopped the conversation, intrigued by the sudden silence that fell among the competitors. All members of the dance committee were now standing facing the dancers. A Cuban national, Mr. Juan S. Gomez, who had recently moved to the country, and then Mr. Carrey approached the future participants. Mr. Carrey buttoned up his jacket. This gesture, emphasized the seriousness of the moment, forcing Solon to straighten up and focus his attention on the two men.

"We are happy to see so many competitors gathered here today," said Mr. Carrey, with a broad smile on his face. "This marathon won't be just any little marathon! 4VRW radio station will be the competition's official station and it will broadcast around the clock everything that will happen during these 100 hours! The most successful businesses in the country have all pledged their support and reserved their advertising spots! It will be a sensational event!"

Solo began to applaud with all his might, not really knowing why. Perhaps, it was Mr. Carrey's enthusiasm that won him over or the promise of the prize. He was already mentally counting the amount that would unlock all the doors for him. Emilio and the rest of the audience follow suit. There was an explosion of applause. Everyone was well aware that this was the first time such a marathon was going to be held in the country.

"We are all as excited as you are! However, the competition has rules that must be followed. Above all, we would like to remind you that this competition will be a test of endurance. Each couple must be physically fit to participate. That is why each registered dancer can have more than one partner."

Mr. Carrey signaled to a young woman with a simple gesture to distribute the numbers.

"You will receive your participant card and your number. This number will identify you and your partners."

As the young woman called out the names, she handed out the numbers. The indiscreet young man sitting in front of Solon was called first. He was named Constantin and received the number 10. Emilio was identified as number 18.

Emilia looked at the card and then at her brother, a knowing smile on her lips. They were in. Emilia opened her bag and slid the card inside to safeguard it.

As the distribution was dragging on a little bit, Shilette was becoming impatient.

"Are you sure you signed up?" she kept on asking Solon.

"Yes... They're calling number 55 now. And the man said there are more than 200 of us participating."

"Then, you must be the 200th," Shilette mocked.

The young woman's sarcastic remark irritated Solon a little. He dug his hand into his pocket to pull out his receipt. He paid the fee and intended to prove it in case they did not give him his number. But the longer he waited, the faster his heart pounded in his chest. Clifford F. Mayer's name was called at 60. He was stiff and upright in his chair. Solon tried to mimic his posture as if it was a token of victory.

Several other names were called in close succession. Solon was still waiting. Worried, he leaned toward Emilio.

"Does your paper look like this?" he asked Emilio in a less assured tone.

Emilio took the receipt and looked at it.

"Yes. It's the same one we have."

Solon put the receipt back in his pocket as his name was finally called.

"Yes!" he said, jumping up from his chair.

The young man fully stretched out his arms to receive the designated number 95. He paid no attention to the stares and the mocking chuckles his gesture drew. He sat back down and held the number tightly in his hands. Weary of losing it, he checked from time to time to make sure it was still there.

Once the last number was assigned, Mr. Gomez continued:

"Every twenty-four hours, women and men will each have an hour to shower and get some sleep before continuing. During the contest, each participant will be entitled to a five-minute break after each hour of dancing. But you can decide to accumulate rest time over two, three, four, five, or six hours. This means that the couple who continually danced, for example, six consecutive hours without a break will be entitled to a thirty-minute break, and so on..."

Emilio's mind quickly assessed the situation. He was becoming increasingly aware of the seriousness of the competition. And above all, he understood the responsibility he had concerning his sister. She was the only companion who could guaranty that the entire check stays in the family. Emilia was not as frail as Marguerite. Unlike Béatrice, who moved slowly, she had energy to spare. However, even though Emilia's wrists and ankles were strong, Emilio had to find a way not to exhaust her.

"If we get thirty minutes of rest after six hours," Emilio whispered in his sister's ear, "that means we can rest for at least sixteen times."

Emilia listened attentively to her brother. Six hours of dancing in a row seemed reasonable. Often, in their small grocery store, she would spend ten hours on her feet helping her mother prepare the goods. At home, when Marguerite had too many soap orders, she would spend the same number of hours helping her. Emilia shook her head in approval. She could do it easily.

"As judges," Mr. Gomez explained, "we have the duty to meticulously record the hours of dancing and the minutes of rest for each participant. We will therefore eliminate any dancer who voluntarily withdraws due to fatigue. This will automatically disqualify that participant and their partners."

Constantin raised his card, which bore the number 10.

"Go ahead," Mr. Carrey encouraged.

"I'd like to know if we're not feeling well, will that disqualify us?"

"It all depends. We will have medical assistance onsite during the 100 hours of the competition. The doctor in charge will be Dr. Wallon, assisted by three nurses from the Department of Medicine at the General Hospital. They will be there to administer massages, showers, vitamins, and other treatments to anyone who need them. But at no time will we encourage anyone to put their life or health at risk to continue in the marathon."

The mention of vitamins surprised Solon and made him laugh furtively. He could not understand what vitamin could automatically give energy to someone. Luckily since he decided to participate, he had already established a regimen. Near Cherilus' house, the merchant who sometimes sold to him on credit, regularly made a broth out of cow's trotters she would buy from the market. Solon, like many people in the neighborhood, knew what day and time the merchant would come around. Therefore, he prepaid the woman to regularly give him a portion through Cherilus who would in turn bring the energy-giving broth to him along with bread that he planned to have Cherilus's wife buy for him.

Solon sat back in his chair, crossing his arms proudly over his chest. All his planning gave him a sense of control. He looked in Clifford F. Mayer's direction. He felt that, just like him, he too was up to the task.

"For the sake of good health," Mr. Gomez announced, "each participant will have their own medical record, which will be given to Dr. Wallon. If you are taking any medication or you are allergic to anything, please don't forget to let us know as soon as this meeting is over."

"Absolutely," Mr. Carrey added. "When the time comes to end the competition, it will be the organizing committee that will decide, based on the criteria we just mentioned, who the winner is. And this decision will be final and without appeal."

Emilio breathed deeply, a sense of calm overtook him. He knew which couple would win. Yet, deep down, he also understood that his victory depended on his endurance. The future of his parents' grocery store depended on the 5,000 *gourdes* ($1,000 USD). Once the debts are paid, they would be able to renovate the store. They would repaint the front walls, change the counter door and allow more customers to enter. On one side, they would keep the grocery store and rent the other. They would install more display cases and raise the shelves to the ceiling, then install an extension ladder. Like the *Nobbe-Bondel* Department Store, they would eventually have a "men's" section selling "*Tropical Anglais*" fabrics, Palm Beach clothing line in every color, beautiful suits at unique prices, a whole range of best quality shirts, ties, handkerchiefs, socks and undershirts. Ladies and young girls who wanted to wear elegant outfits would find the prettiest embroideries fashioned by Marguerite and cotton lace plus a whole assortment of *crêpe* fabrics...

As her brother was planning the future, a young woman sitting a little further on the left caught Emilia's attention. That woman stood out among the competitors. Her glasses large dark frame made her look enigmatic. Her name was Adrienne Dolan.

Emilia stared at her with growing interest, realizing that, unlike her, she was not just a partner. She was the main character in her story. She was number 27.

CHAPTER 5
The Idea that saved them

Augustin and Christian were not present at the meeting. Christian could not convince his mother about his participation. Finding support with other upper-class families in boycotting the dance competition, it was she who announced to him that Franco Francini's parents, offended by their son being at such an event, requested that his name to be removed from the list of participants.

This news was felt like a wind storm that plunged Augustin into deep despair. He thought about the developing situation: he could find himself at odds with Marie-Agnès if his insistence in participating in the competition went against Mrs. Grégoire's wishes. That was one thing he could not bear.

However, unlike Augustin, Christian persisted.

"We're not children!" he reminded him. "My participation can't depend on my parents' permission! Is this Franco Francini a man or a wimp?! This is the first time such an event is taking place in the country! Even the sisal company we work for has decided to sponsor the competition just because we're going to participate."

"Yes," Augustin interrupted, "but I don't see the point in us having any kind of problem with our families just for that..."

Annoyed by his friend's lack of a back bone, Christian watched him scratch his neck with a doubtful and worried expression. He felt sorry for Augustin every time he saw him in such depressive mood. Life in post-war Port-au-Prince was offering so many new activities and Christian wanted to experience them all.

"Okay," he finally said. "I'll think of another plan. In the meantime, since we missed the meeting at the club, I got our numbers. Here. You're number 31 and I'm number 30."

Augustin took the numbered card without much enthusiasm. He looked thoughtfully at the number 31 written in bold. Looking down at the floor, he rubbed the card against his pants as if this gesture would help him find a way out. What if, as Mrs. Grégoire pointed out, their participation in this competition degraded their surname? What if, through his fault, his father lost the fine reputation he had built up over so many years in the tourism industry? Was the swift action of Francini senior warranted? Maybe that was why he went to the newspaper himself and made sure that the announcement of his son's withdrawal was published.

A saddened Augustin parted ways with his friend, wandering down the street, completely absorbed in thought. Everything that was usually familiar to him in the neighborhood seemed like the setting of a foreign film noir.

The Montrose home was a two-story Gingerbread house painted sage green with façade walls made of beige brick. Large pillars supported the front porch and its roof and gave an appearance of grandeur to the home. The rectangular porch, though spacious, did not wrap around the house like that of the Grégoires. While the main staircase started on one side, a huge, mature orange bougainvillea was blocking part of the entrance, shielding it from the view of passersby.

Augustin climbed the stairs with heavy steps and threw himself onto the first chair he found. As always, he reflects on the best course of action to take; this attitude shielded him from many mistakes in the past. So why did he listen to Christian this time and entered this competition without thinking? If he had not rushed into it, he would have known that Marie-Agnès received a scholarship. He would have understood it was the perfect time to pour out his heart to her. But instead, he found himself at the center of a family disagreement! If he had refused to enter the competition, he would have risked a falling out with his friend. However, as he did, he was risking now offending Marie-Agnès's parents, thereby ruining any possibility of a union with her.

Augustin leaned on his elbow, a fist under his jaw, wanting to scream.

"Is something wrong?" his father asked hoarsely.

The young man jumped in surprise. When he entered, he did not notice his father sitting behind the bougainvillea.

"What are you doing here, Dad? I thought you were welcoming tourists at the Wharf?"

"I'm feeling unwell," he replied and sneezed into a handkerchief. "Abel went to meet them. I'll see them tomorrow morning, maybe."

"Abel is definitely the best assistant you ever had."

"Without a doubt. I can count on him at any time."

"Anyway, if you still feel sick tomorrow, there's no point in bothering him. I'll go for you, Dad. They need to start getting used to my face."

"That would be nice. I need some rest," replied his father with his eyes reddened by fatigue and weakness.

Joseph Montrose looked proudly at his son. With refined manners, a straight stance in his cream jacket, what a man he had become! How he did not regret his strictness back then when Augustin who was studying abroad, begged him to return home. The horrors of World War II raging across Europe had unsettled him. However, Mr. Montrose knew that in Switzerland his son was safe. Moreover, he was with Christian. He was not alone. So, he insisted that he continues his studies until graduation. Those years in Switzerland certainly transformed Augustin. From a fearful boy, his son grew into a twenty-three-year-old man that he could count on to soon take over his travel agency.

Upon his return to Haiti, his son would have already put his skills to good use in the family business. But Mr. Montrose wanted Augustin to completely skirt his future duties. He wanted him to see the uncertain and disappointing life the masses lead in his own country; the sisal factory on the outskirts of the city offered the best archetype of these struggles. Joseph Montrose was preparing his son to the challenges he would undoubtedly face when he would take over the agency.

The family's travel agency was indeed a perfect example of earned victories. It was a testament to resilience, tenacity, and faith in the future. In the turmoil of World War II, when bankruptcies were multiplying and layoffs were a daily occurrence, Joseph Montrose and his wife kept all their staff. They encouraged them during the slow economy to master the English language as best they could. He and his wife were convinced that things would not remain this way indefinitely…

"How's the building's expansion coming along, Dad?"

"It's nearing the finishing stage. We installed the doors and windows yesterday. You should see the flood of natural light now streaming into the rooms! I think by the end of March, we'll be able to start furnishing it according to the designs your mother and you came up with."

"By then, I'll have already handed in my resignation at the factory, and Mom will be back."

"Indeed... I can't wait for you to come work with us, son."

Augustin smiled approvingly as he got up from his chair. He touched his father's arm as he passed by before briefly entering the living room.

The living room was spacious, furnished in the Art Deco style. The sharply angled furniture coexisted in perfect harmony with the curved furniture, conveying a comfortable feel. This living room departed from the Haitian *bourgeoisie's* esthetic who embraced the French style of the last century. This difference was intentional. Augustin's parents sought to remind themselves and any guest who entered their home, that their family was looking toward the future.

Augustin walked over to a semicircular mahogany bar cabinet. He opened both doors and first scanned the selection of bottles in front of him. He chose a mint liqueur and poured the emerald-colored drink into a crystal glass.

"Would you like some liqueur, Dad?" he shouted from inside the house. "It'll warm your lungs and put an end to that cold!"

"I'd prefer some *kremas,* if there's any left."

Augustin prepared the drinks and returned to the porch. The scent of rhum, coconut milk, and the spices that made up the rich, creamy *kremas* tickled his nostrils. He almost regretted choosing the mint liqueur, which had a dry taste.

"We have a large bottle of *kremas,*" he said, handing the glass to his father. "I think I'll have some too in a bit. It smells so good."

The young man moved his chair closer to his father's before slowly sitting down. As he raised his head, his face became thoughtful again. He stared blindly at his glass, remaining silent. His internal turmoil had returned.

"What's going on?" ask Joseph Montrose who noticed his son's distant gaze. "Lately, your mood seemed to be swinging. One time you look sad, the next you are happy. Is it the sisal company?"

"No," replied Augustin, his voice flat.

"What is it then?"

Augustin looked back at his father. Why had he never shared with him his love for Marie-Agnès? Was it the fear of being misunderstood, or simply the fear of appearing vulnerable by revealing his deepest feelings?

"Dad, do you know about the dance marathon?" he asked.

"It's all the talk at the agency! In fact, we're even planning to invite some travel journalists to attend."

"So, you're not against it?" asked Augustin.

"Not at all. It's a "great event", as they call it in the newspapers. And it will bring a lot of excitement to the *Cité de l'Exposition* (Expo City)."

"Christian and I signed up last week."

"Really?" Mr. Montrose asked in surprise. "I didn't know you were interested... It seems to be a trend that's spreading throughout the Caribbean. Puerto Rico is currently holding a similar competition. Theirs will last 20 days and that's 500 hours."

"Good God!" Augustin said in surprise.

Joseph Montrose slowly took a sip of his creamy beverage and flashed a sly smile.

"You know, some friends and I once took part in a similar competition in New York in the 1920s. That one lasted two weeks. But we gave up before the end!"

"You, in a walkathon?" Augustin asked in surprise.

"Well, it was the Roaring Twenties!" his father replied, his eyes shining with happiness at the memories. "It was the swing era! We were young and full of energy!"

Mr. Montrose visibly went back in his mind. He was tapping his feet and snapping his fingers. The sound was so vivid in his ears that he closed his eyes for a moment and hummed the tune.

"Ah!" he said, laughing. "Those little gliding steps, the endless improvisations, especially if your partner played along! And then, when you were caught up in the whirlwind of the dance, you'd make the girl jump in the air! You'd twirl her around!"

Augustin heard his father's bursts of laughter, but was unable to share his enthusiasm. Yes, his father was happily lost in his own mind, however, Christian mother's voice was echoing in Augustin's head. His friend's mother warning tone was contrasted to his father's remembered joy.

"The Grégoires are against it," Augustin said nervously. "They think our participation in such a degrading competition could tarnish our reputation."

Joseph Montrose rolled his eyes. Now, he understood why Roger Grégoire has been wanting to talk to him so urgently for the past few days.

"First of all, it's not degrading. Gomez and Carrey are well-known event planners and they have had successful ones to their credit already; and this dance marathon will be just another. Imagine the 100 hours of non-stop dancing! It's a test that will bring out the resilience of our people! Secondly, I don't see how our reputation could be tarnished. The echo of our rich culture is vibrating in every corner of the world. Our family lives in a country that is attracting more people, becoming one of the biggest destinations of this post-war period! Seasoned Haitian musicians will provide entertainment for four days. In the idyllic setting of *Les Palmistes*, this competition will attract many more people and make headlines, as it has already, even though it hasn't even started yet."

Mr. Montrose let out a mocking laugh.

"Degrading? Come on now!"

But Augustin's father paused. His approval was not enough for his son apparently. There was something else bothering Augustin. Silently, Mr. Montrose continued sipping his *kremas,* giving the young man the time he needed to open up.

Augustin leaned back in his chair, one arm resting loosely on the armrest. He was emotionally exhausted. Instead of uplifting him, his father's words added to his burden. The sum of his fears was intertwined with his undisclosed love; that love was risking to take a severe blow if he found himself face to face with the Grégoires.

"Dad!" he finally blurted out. "You don't understand. If I participate, I'll lose her!"

Joseph Montrose remained silent a moment.

"Tell me, why do you want to participate?" he finally asked.

Augustin did not know what to say. Christian and himself just talked about it as a challenge, a way to test their endurance. However, confronted to his father's question, this logic suddenly seemed bland. Those four days of dancing were a waste compared to the short time he had to seduce Marie-Agnès before she left for Austria. Augustin's silence forced Mr. Montrose to frown.

"I know I've told this story more than once to both you and your sister; but listen to it one more time... Our family didn't receive anything on a silver platter. My father's countryside shop in the city of *Pestel* couldn't afford to pay for a higher education abroad after I received a basic education in Port-au-Prince. So, I had to turn to outside sources. To earn a full scholarship to study hospitality in New York in the early 1910s, I had to stay up late at night, often by lamplight, and study relentlessly. Once in New York, my dual mission was to bring home a degree and make my family proud. I had an unwavering goal to succeed and climb the social ladder. And…I…I did it. We did it. Today, we are part of this Haitian *bourgeoisie*... Listen, my son. If you find a good reason to participate in this competition, believe me, Marie-Agnès will look at you differently. In her eyes, you will not only become a symbol of courage, but she will also see in you a man of convictions who is not afraid to make sacrifices to defend them."

Suddenly, Augustin straightened up, looking at his father in surprise. He did not mention her once. How had he guessed who his heart was beating for?

Augustin's father coughed a little, then added:

"Your mother and I figured it for a long time. You never missed an opportunity to be near her. When you were very young, I took a lot of pictures of you all; the Volmar girls, the Grégoires, your sister, and you were almost inseparable. In all of them, you were never far away when she was present. When you were studying in Switzerland, not a letter, not a telegram, came without asking how she was doing..."

As his father shared his observations, Augustin's eyes grew increasingly misty with tears. He placed his glass slowly on the tile; his trembling hands made the crystal clang against the floor. His deeply buried feelings have been unmasked. His love laid bare. Two tears fell freely. He never thought his father could understand him so well. He felt a lump in his throat. So many years of repressed emotions were rising inside him like the crater of a boiling volcano. He leaned down on his knees, clutched his head in his hands, and sobbed like a child.

Though sitting upright with a dignified head, Joseph Montrose was tearing also. He was sharing his son's pain and distress. But he remained glued to his chair. He was not the type to hug and show visible affection.

"Come on now," he said calmly with a breaking voice. "You know, I felt the same way since the first day I saw your mother. However, I had to fight to have her by my side. Life is a struggle! If it's Marie-Agnès who makes your heart flutter, if she's the one who will make you happy for the rest of your life, fight for her, my son! Fight!"

Augustin stayed on the porch for a long time, shedding tears. His pain kept him captive for so long. He could no longer kept at bay waves and waves of emotional desperation. The feelings were rising deep from within him. So many years of repressed passions fed every ugly sob, every cry.

His father, in front of such a scene, did not dare to add anything. He understood that Augustin needed this relief. His own eyes were misty. He felt every bit of his son's pain as if his story was also his.

That evening, when the young man was finally resting in his bedroom, he took out an envelope from a drawer. It was in it that he kept a collection of concert programs that Marie-Agnès had ever performed in. He laid them on his bed. With swollen eyes, he looked at them one after the other. He remembered every recital; every bouquet of flowers he ever sent her. Sleep finally overcame Augustin as he searched in his mind for something that would help him fight.

"Fight for her!" he recalled his father advised him.

The next day, Augustin woke up with a renew vigor he never felt before. Now that he voiced his feelings, he was sure about what he needed to do. His reason to participate was obvious. His heart would power him to the success he desires.

At breakfast, Augustin shared his taught with his father.

"Go ahead," Mr. Montrose agreed, his expression proud.

"Thanks, Dad... How are you feeling this morning?"

"Still tired..."

"I can meet those tourists if you want, like I promised yesterday."

"No. It's not necessary. I've already sent a message to Abel. He'll go meet them ... Fully focus on your goal now."

Augustin touched his father's hands, pleased with this complicity. He quickly ate his breakfast while starting to work on his plan. He did not want to drop by Christian's house unannounced. He wanted his visit to be a bit more serious; he did not want his idea to be trivialized.

The young man picked up the phone and dialed four numbers.

"Have you found anything?" Christian asked as soon as he realized who was calling.

"Yes! Let me explain to you..."

Christian let out a small sigh as he listened to his friend. He was not sure about the idea. He thought it was too serious for him. All he wanted was to have fun. His participation in the dance competition did not require such an elaborate scheme.

"We'll see," Christian said unenthusiastically. "Come around five o'clock. Everyone would awaken from their nap. We'll be gathered on the porch."

The wait was torture to Augustin. He could not stop sighing loudly, constantly calling the housekeeper for insignificant matters. He called her from the living room while leafing through travel magazines; he asked for her in his room while on his bed trying to read the Creole poem collection he just bought; he called her to the courtyard while chatting with the staff. Augustin was acting crazy and he was driving his father insane.

Joseph Montrose was indeed tired of all the commotion. Every time he wanted to rest, the creaking of the wooden floor under Augustin's nervous footsteps echoed throughout the house. When it was finally closed to five o'clock, Mr. Montrose emerged from his siesta and advised his son to go to the Grégoires.

Wasting no more time, Augustin snatched his jacket off the back of a chair in the living room, grabbed his hat, and hurried on the street. The closer he was getting to the Grégoires' house, the more heightened his senses were; the short distance he had to walk felt like hundreds of miles.

Marie-Agnès and her sister were not on the porch when he arrived. Christian was talking to his parents about the plan of opening the guesthouse jointly with Augustin's father. Yet, despite the exchanges, Christian's mind was elsewhere. He was eager to see how his friend's idea would be interpreted by his parents, even though his mother's reaction no longer had a sway on his mind. With his number 30 in hand and his partners already chosen, he was determined to take part in the competition regardless.

The sounds of footsteps on the gravel and then on the main staircase caught everyone's attention.

"Ah!" said Mr. Grégoire when he saw Augustin. "Your father is nowhere to be found lately."

"He was very busy this week with a group of students from the countryside. Their school wanted them to visit some of the city's monuments, including the exhibition site."

"That's true," confirmed Mr. Grégoire. "He told me so the last time we spoke."

"Yes, but he has been under the weather since yesterday."

"A lot of people seem to be affected by this cold these days," observed Mrs. Grégoire. "We're in a drought, and the temperature is cool in the evenings. A heat and cold created the perfect environment for sickness! I'll give you a syrup that might help him."

"Thank you," said Augustin, looking a little concerned. "I'm sure it'll help him along with all the tea the housekeeper makes for him."

"Your father works too much!" pointed out Mrs. Grégoire. "He needs to rest a little."

"That's exactly what I told him yesterday. But he's already thinking about his schedule for next week. He wants to get better as quickly as possible so he can accompany some journalists he met in Florida to the dance competition."

Elsa Grégoire stared surprisingly at Augustin. A look of incomprehension flashed on her face.

"And... he knows you'll be participating?" she asked.

"Yes," the young man replied, standing up suddenly.

Marie-Agnès and her sister were joining them on the porch. They were walking joyfully arm in arm. With each slow, light steps, Marie-Agnès brought with her a floatable scent of lavender. Her fresh complexion was contained in a cotton dress. She was girded by a silk ribbon which showed her well-proportioned body. Her short dark brown hair was pulled back with a tortoiseshell hair comb clip which completed her attractive aura. Augustin watched her, fascinated by this simplicity that nevertheless was hiding an unparalleled intelligence. Marie-Cécile kissed Augustin on the cheek while her sister simply waved before sitting down on a *dodine* (a rocking chair). The young man tried to remain calm and struggle to take his eyes off Marie-Agnès.

"And doesn't your father mind if his name is tarnished by this thing?" Mrs. Grégoire continued, as if she did not notice Augustin's fascination with her daughter.

"Well," Augustin replied ingenuously, "he assured me that our reputation will remain intact, especially since it will be for a good cause."

"A cause?" Marie-Cécile asked intriguingly. "What is it?"

Christian leaned against the railing, arms crossed over his chest, eyes shining with excitement, eagerly awaiting his parents' reaction. He could see the stress on his friend's face as he tried his best to find the right words.

"This participation will benefit the Tuberculosis Sanatorium of Port-au-Prince," Augustin revealed in a whisper. “What's being done there to care for all these poor people means a lot to me...”

“That's an excellent idea,” Marie-Agnès cheered with a small smile.

Augustin's heart leaped, realizing he just caught the attention of his beloved. Usually, she barely participated in the conversations he was involved in. And now, her words were accompanied by a smile...

“You volunteered at the Sanatorium last year, didn’t you?” Christian asked his older sister.

“Yes. It was a deep experience...” Marie-Agnès replied.

Mrs. Grégoire stared at Augustin with a suspicious look, while everyone around her seemed charmed by the young man's idea.

“And why is it only now that you are sharing this?” she asked.

“Mom,” Christian interjected, trying to shield his friend from her pointed inquiry, “you were so against it that Augustin had to make sure first we wouldn't do anything stupid.”

“That's true, Mrs. Grégoire. When you mentioned it was degrading, I admit I spent nights thinking about it;

because dragging our surname through the mud is the last thing Christian and I would want to happen."

"But, Mom, why did you think that?" Marie-Agnès objected gently. "I worked for a month in that sanatorium and never in my life have I seen a disease like this! Tuberculosis is one of the country's greatest plagues!"

As she spoke, an enormous sadness crossed the young woman's face. The vivid images of that trying experience came back to her in all their desperate afflictions.

"I assure you," Marie-Agnès continued, "they need all the funds they can find to continue the fight against tuberculosis."

"Absolutely," Augustin replied eagerly. "And it was this awareness that drove us to want to give our energy to support this hospital."

Mr. Grégoire smoothed his mustache. He remembered how, without the Sanatorium, tuberculosis could have wiped out the Haitian population. The empirical remedies that families were administering to their sick ones were causing the infection rate to increase day by day. Shame was also causing the families to hide and abandon their sick ones to death. How many employees from the Department of Finance lost a loved one, when it was not their own life! It was for this reason that he had been among those who supported the construction of the medical facility from the very start.

"Your mother and I were there on the day of the inauguration," Mr. Grégoire said to Christian. "And if I'm not mistaken, I believe your parents were there too, Augustin."

"Yes. They told me about that wonderful evening."

"This is quite an achievement for Dr. Roy! He is the one who introduced an effective treatment for the disease in the country."

"Well, Augustin, your possible participation will be the most generous gesture," declared Marie-Agnès, looking admiringly at the young man.

Augustin swallowed and smiled stupidly. The praise made his body heat up, causing a buzzing sensation in his ears as his heart rate accelerated. His wise father was right. His idea made him more appealing to Marie-Agnès.

Mr. Grégoire also looked at Augustin with more interest. He, then, embarked on a philosophic soliloquy about the need to help the country move forward. He highlighted the current extraordinary Haitian minds that are shining brightly around the world but he lamented the many others whom with untaped potentials are languishing in ignorance and darkness.

"The economic health of a country lays above all on the physical and mental health of its people!" he declared.

"Absolutely," Augustin added. "This question of physical health is a real leitmotif for Dr. Roy."

"Rumor has it," said Marie-Agnès, "that other wings are going to be opened at the Sanatorium".

"This is fantastic!" exclaimed Mr. Grégoire. "An increase in the number of beds is crucial."

"You're right, Dad," admitted Marie-Agnès. "The air is very pure on *Morne l'Hôpital*'s hill. It will help these patients whom are accustomed to live in the heat of the city's overcrowded suburbs."

Christian was following the discussion with unwavering interest, dazzled by the efficacity of his friend's plan. He felt that his parents' sentiment toward the dance contest was changing. His father's enthusiasm surprised him; and his mother's sterned features gradually were relaxing.

"So, you won't mind if I, along with Augustin, participate in this noble cause?" he asked.

Elsa Grégoire adjusted her skirt and crossed her legs. All things considered, her son's participation could be a great credit to their family. A philanthropist reputation might be useful in the future.

"We won't mind," she agreed casually. "I'm all for helping the needy to the best of our ability. You are both young. Spending your energy this way is a good thing."

Augustin's ears resonated in amazement. All the anxiety he felt in engineering the scheme and not knowing how it would be accepted vanished away. This reversal of opinion from Christian's parents and Marie-Agnès's support made his eyes shine with amorous hope. In an aura of profound happiness, he breathed deeply. Yes, this excellent cause he intended to win it. He was going to win for the health of the nation. He was going to win for those suffering of tuberculosis. He was going to win Marie-Agnès' heart.

CHAPTER 6
The Hour has come

Augustin could hardly contain himself in the days before the start of the competition. His impatience was so palpable that his father had to remind him continually that he needed to relax and build up his strength for the 100 hours that were awaiting him.

On the evening of the start of the event, the weather forecast called for a bright and cloudless sky. The venue's sign glittered under the silver night. A large billboard advertised the contest in French, English, and Spanish, attracting this way many tourists visiting the garden of the *Palmistes* area.

With a small duffel bag in hand, Augustin anxiously entered the venue while Christian, on the other hand, was casually carrying his. They arrived just as Mr. Gomez, standing in the middle of the dance floor, flanked by two men and two women, was giving direct instructions to the contestants.

"I hope no one forgot to bring extra clothes for the four days," he said. "Remember that every morning before

6:00 a.m., you can go to the restrooms in groups to wash up. The women's restrooms are located very close to the women's section. The men's quarters will be on the other side. Upon entering your respective areas, you will find camp beds that a store kindly donated to us. Take advantage of them to rest during the time allotted to you. As we told you during the last meeting, we have not planned on feeding you. We hope your families will take care of that. It's six o'clock, kids! The Show is at nine o'clock sharp!"

Mr. Gomez looked at his watch as to signal the importance of this point in time and concluded his speech.

The participants dispersed noisily as Christian and Augustin looked around, searching for their partners. They took a few steps towards the women's section. No one was there.

"I hope they didn't stand us up," Christian said frowningly.

"Did you remind them of the time?" Augustin asked worriedly.

"Yes..."

Augustin's anxiety rose a notch. Without partners, he and his friend would be eliminated from the start. The mere thought of it gave the young man a slight headache.

Christian and Augustin entered the men's quarters and chose two beds against a wall at the very back of the room. They placed their bags and a carboard box with their names on it. Then they headed back to the dance floor.

This marathon was Augustin's whole life at that precise moment. He could not see his future without the 5,000 *gourdes* check which he was going to hand over to the Sanatorium. He gave his word, after all. Christian and he were not going to only participate but they were aiming to win. It was a must.

"Well!" said a voice on Christian back. "Here we are finally competing in a dance contest!"

"Max Belmont!" said Christian.

The two young men embraced in a burst of laughter and patted each other on the back loudly. Christian and Augustin have not seen Max for several months. With the responsibility to coordinate all shipments for the family import-export company, the Belmont Terminals Limited, Max had no time to be seen at dance clubs. But as a bon-vivant, he couldn't miss this event.

"As usual, we'll have to be faithful to our custom of being the last to leave the dance floor!" reminded Max.

"You bet!" Augustin replied with a broad smile.

Another young man, in his thirties, was standing behind him and smiling.

"Oh!" said Max, trying to tame his ruffled hair. "This is Clifford F. Mayer. A childhood friend and an expert in dance marathons."

"Fantastic!" replied Christian as he shook Mayer's hand. "Another walkathon lover!"

The four burst out in laughter.

"So, your parents let you participate without a lecture?" asked Max.

"Well…," said Christian. "We got one, but they finally gave in since we're doing it for the benefit of the Sanatorium."

"Impressive," admired Max Belmont, patting Christian on the shoulder.

"Well done!" congratulated Mayer.

Tall and almost skeletal, Max Belmont looked at his watch and touched his flat stomach.

"We're going to eat at the *Carillon*. Are you joining us?"

"No, sorry," replied Augustin quickly, almost being overcome with apprehension. "Our partners haven't arrived yet and…"

"Neither have ours," Mayer interrupted. "You know women. They're always late."

"He's right," admitted Christian. "I'm sure they'll be here when we get back."

Even though Augustin was hungry, he followed the group reluctantly. He was not in the mood for a party. Their casualness was irritating him a little as he wondered about the possibility of his elimination. But as he was leaving the venue apprehensively, he bumped into Agathe and Mireille, who were finally arriving.

"Good God! Where have you both been?" Augustin reproached.

The two twenty-two-year-old women seemed to be in no hurry. They were even surprised by Augustin's question. Mireille stared at him with dismissive eyes.

"Hey!... We had to eat and rest," she replied.

Agathe and Mireille were carrying large suitcases filled with the toiletries and clothing they would need for the next four days.

"Let us help you," offered Christian.

"No, no, it's fine," replied Agathe hurriedly. "We'll see you later."

Unexpectedly, one of the venue's doormen rudely reached and grabbed the luggage. The move left Christian and Augustin a bit surprised as they intended to help the girls to the women's section.

Relieved by the presence of their partners, Augustin took a deep breath. He turned and followed his friends, who were already starting to walk towards the restaurant located a few minutes away.

In front of the club entrance, a small line of supporters was waiting for some time. Parents and friends of the participants, who bought their tickets weeks in advance, were elbowing each other to find a good spot in front of the stage. Two men, in simple black suits, pointed to a large sign that read: "reserved area". Decorated with red hibiscus flowers and oleanders, the front rows aroused the curiosity of many.

"Why aren't they letting us sit on this side?" protested a woman in her forties, accompanied by a few family members. "We bought four tickets and we can't sit wherever we want?!"

"They must be reserved for foreigners," explained one of her sons, barely fourteen years old.

"Yes, but we also spent a lot of money to attend the contest even though we don't know any of the participants!" replied her sister.

"Calm down," demanded their uncle. "At least we have a seat near the front, even if it's not the one close to the musicians."

The woman, in her forties, mumbled a few words while arranging the family's lunch in a bag. Like many of the fans that evening who intended to stay for a little while, she brought sandwiches, cookies, and drinks that would last until the early hours of the next morning.

This group of early spectators inside the club were in no way bothered by the final preparations they were witnessing before the start of the marathon.

Around 8:30 pm, Joseph Montrose slipped through the crowd, accompanied by Abel, his assistant, as well as three travel-and-leisure journalists from Florida. The small group sat on straw chairs around a table set up on an island transformed into a restaurant. The evening was barely beginning for them. Joseph Montrose wanted the reporters, who were sojourning in the capital, to experience first the dance marathon. Then, they would savor a *griot,* the typical national dish (marinaded, spicy fried pork meat served with other fried sides dishes and a hot sauce).

The journalists took in the scene with enchanted eyes. All around the nightclub there were islets connected by small wooden bridges. The waters of the Gulf of *La Gonâve* meandered between them, reflecting the silhouettes of oleanders, tree ferns, and a forest of giant palm trees. Spotlights were showcasing trees on which were hung the marathon's regulations, written in three languages. One of the journalists closed his eyes to breathe in the sea air and to better feel the breeze which was gently stirring the palm leaves. Another sketched a diagram of the club and noted the tropical shrubs and flowers surrounding it.

Mr. Montrose was happily yet calmly following them from the corner of his eye. He knew what this first impression would mean for his business. Once the journalists returned to their country, the columns they would write in the cultural sections of their respective magazines and newspapers would attract even more tourists.

"I've always heard about these marathons," one of the reporters said excitedly in French with a heavy English accent. "But this is the first time I'll see one in person."

"It's a first in our country. And I have a feeling it's going to be amazing..." Mr. Montrose responded.

"We love dancing!" informed Abel. "From infancy, dancing is part of everything we do."

"That's true," Mr. Montrose confirmed. "For us, dance is more than just a hobby. It's the very soul of our country."

"The very soul, you say?" asked another journalist while opening his notebook.

"It is through our dances that we express ourselves and celebrate life. Our dances have a deep connection to our history. Each of them tells its own story, influenced by the African traditions that the slaves brought to the island," Mr. Montrose explained.

"With the bicentennial celebration of Port-au-Prince," Abel said, "the Department of Tourism took the opportunity to showcase our traditional dances from the countryside; the public performances will be held mainly at the *Théâtre de Verdure*."

"But tonight, at the marathon launch," Mr. Montrose clarified, "you won't see any dances with spiritual connotations. You will surely hear music that highlights festive dances like the bolero or the *méringue*..."

"Merengue, you mean?" the intrigued journalist interrupted.

"No," Abel corrected. "It's not merengue dance like in Spanish, but *méringue*, a music that originated from the colony."

The assistant began to beat the time on the table.

"Our *méringue* has five beats per measure. Like this," he said.

One of the journalists followed the assistant's lead and tried to reproduce the rhythm.

"Ah! You're talented," Abel congratulated.

"Bravo!" Mr. Montrose encouraged. "All these rhythms emerged with the arrival of the slaves. Overtime, they mixed with the colonists' own musical offerings on the island of *Saint-Domingue*. Many of them, like the *carabinier* or the *djouba*, for example, are the slaves' response to French culture."

"Interesting... But you also dance Spanish music, right?"

"Absolutely," Abel affirmed. "We have excellent relations with the Spanish-speaking countries around us, which means we're no strangers to salsa or rumba…"

"It's a shame we're leaving tomorrow," said one of the journalists. "We'll have to come back and explore further this part of your culture."

"Excellent idea!" Mr. Montrose agreed.

"How about we immortalize this moment?" Abel suggested.

The assistant adjusted Mr. Montrose's Kodak camera while the latter joined the group of journalists who were placing their notebooks and own cameras away on the table.

The four men huddled together for the photo and smiled broadly.

Mr. Carrey, standing near the technicians of the radio station 4VRW, noticed the presence of Joseph Montrose. Even though he knew him through his travel agency, he was pressed by the tasks he had to finish before the start of the marathon. The organizer cracked a smile before leaning over to the chief reporter.

"You have the list of the sponsors, don't you?" he asked.

"Yes," confirmed the chief commentator while consulting the list of about ten businesses.

"Could you add John Haig Whisky, Pontiac dealership, and Curaçao Trading?" Mr. Carrey asked before leaving.

"Sure."

The contest's official radio station was ready for its first live broadcast. One of the assistants manning the radio's studio mixers made a 'ready' signal to the chief commentator who waited for the producer's countdown: four... three... two...

"Dear listeners, good evening! You're tuned in on 4VRW, the competition's official radio! We're live from the *Palmistes*! The dance competition will begin in an hour. I can say it has been already a euphoric atmosphere! The participants are ready! The musicians of the *Orchestre Caraïbes* are looking great in their costumes and are just waiting for the signal! Come see this extraordinary show, which is being held for the first time in Haiti! Come support the dancers, and why not, come dance yourself! Admission is only 1 *gourde* ($0.20 USD)! There are very few seats left! Don't miss this sensational four-day event, which is taking place right here at the *Palmiste*! Come day or night! Come see our country's most famous musicians and tenacious dancers!"

The chief commentator gestured he finished his announcement to the technicians. Around him, the organizers' assistants were still busy. Some of them were responsible for ensuring that all the spectators, especially those who were gathering at the club entrance, could enter and cheer their favorite competitors.

The line of fans, stretching out into the street, included a few European and South American tourists in summer attire, looking for excitement. Cherilus and Rosa were standing behind one of them. Of Solon's acquaintances, they were the only ones who managed to get in without spending a dime of their meager income. Despite the fatigue caused by their daily obligations, the two offered their services to help clean the venue, thus securing a spot.

While Cherilus and Rosa were still in line, around 8:45p.m., the unmistakable honking of official vehicles sounded. The arrival of these black Buicks with Dynaflow in front of the nightclub attracted attention. Several officers got out first to form a security perimeter, while a few others pushed back people who were too close to the club's entrance. Rapidly, the welcoming committee, led by the marathon's organizers, positioned themselves in front of the club. Heads held high, straight postures, smiles on their faces, they waited.

A few local and foreign journalists rushed to take pictures of the attending officers and the welcoming committee before turning their cameras on a car that was just pulling up. One of them waited for a few seconds while the journalists' camera flashes continued to go off. An officer finally opened the door and very carefully helped a passenger out.

"Oh! It's her," Cherilus recognized.

A whisper rose in the air as a few amazed people applauded.

"Who's she?" asked Rosa.

"The First Lady..."

Rosa's short stature was unkind to her in this situation. She moved slightly out of line to get a better look at the President's wife. So many times, she missed the First Lady while she accompanied her presidential husband during his frequent visits to the construction of the various sections of the Expo City.

"Thank you for honoring us with your fine presence, Madame Estimé," said Mr. Gomez and courteously kissed her hand.

"I had to come and see with my own eyes the launch of this distinctive competition!"

The First Lady walked toward the club. She passed by Cherilus and the men who were standing in line. The men removed their hats to greet her and show respect. All the women present looked on admiringly at the First Lady's dressed in an elegant pale suit. The government officials surrounded Mrs. Estimé protectively as she briefly greeted the crowd with a smile.

Inside, all the spectators rose from their seats, applauding the arrival of the President's wife. She thanked them with great satisfaction and randomly shook a few hands.

Dr. Wallon, the physician in charge of the emergency service, was also part of the welcoming committee. He proudly led the First Lady to his medical area that was set up strategically between the dance floor and the competitors' quarters. Mrs. Estimé made a brief inspection, congratulating him. The doctor indeed well-organized participants' medical records, first aid equipment and materials were skillfully displayed.

"Dr. Wallon, you are, without a doubt, the best choice for this competition," praised the First Lady.

"I'm flattered, Your Excellency," replied the doctor. "Fortunately, I have qualified nurses at my side to carry out successfully this task entrusted to me."

Three nurses came forward and bowed discreetly.

"These are young ladies who have a true love for their profession and are experienced in the noble work they will be doing," Dr. Wallon continued.

"We will therefore have," observed the First Lady, "a marathon that I hope will be remembered by generations to come."

"Without a doubt, Your Excellency," Mr. Carrey agreed.

Meanwhile, from both the men's and women's quarters, participants rushed to the door to see what caused the roaring applauses.

"Mrs. Estimé is here!" Constantin informed excitedly with his number 10 well affixed on his back.

The participants who were off-stage came also running, standing on their tiptoes to get a better look.

"She's even more beautiful in real life!" said one person admiringly.

The presence of Mrs. Estimé and the other officials made an impression on Emilio. His heart race a little faster as he leaned on Solon's Shoulder. He had never met the president or his wife. This presence added value and solemnity to the dance marathon that he or his family never expected.

"I wonder if she'll stay until the end..."

"She'll be the one to give us the check," affirmed a competitor standing next to Emilio.

Solon nodded in approval, his eyes scanning the packed room, and feeling excited. Finally, the anticipated moment arrived. He thought that, he, Solon, a provincial boy from the southern part of the country, was officially in a dance marathon among the refined people of the capital, and especially in front of the illustrated Mrs. Estimé. His parents would have been so proud of him.

"You have ten minutes before going on the dance floor!" one of the assistants shouted from the men's section.

Emilio's ears tingled with the announcement. He felt butterflies in his stomach. He closed his eyes for a moment and breathed in deeply, then exhaled. Both he and his sister practiced this relaxation exercise many times for this very occasion. Emilio stretched his neck in all directions, repeatedly letting his arms fall to his sides.

Solon watched Emilio and tried copying his movements. He too felt the rising pressure and was clenching his jaw with anxiety. He could not stop wringing his hands to calm himself down and to warm his now cold fingers. He would soon begin the competition of his life. All his dreams and future were resting on these hundred hours. Solon inspected his clothes and touched his back to make sure the number 95 was firmly attached to it.

From his camp bed, this gesture amused Christian. He looked at Solon and noted his arched posture, his thick hands, his wide-opened eyes. Christian then looked around at the other participants. Clifford F. Mayer was standing with his legs apart, his arms crossed over his chest, the number 60 on his back, talking with Max Belmont, number 55. Their confidence was contrasting with that of a few other men who were overly impressed by the event. Christian smiled. He was suddenly realizing that, besides city dwellers, country folks were also taking part in this competition.

"I have a feeling we're going to have a lot of fun," he said.

With a distant gaze, Augustin barely heard the remark. He was in another world insulated from the surrounding excitement. He was thinking about Marie-Agnès and was imagining what would be her reaction when he would hand over the check to the Sanatorium's director. Would she be proud of him? Would he have the opportunity to tell her how he feels about her? Augustin ran his hands over his face. The stress made him feel nauseous for a moment.

"We have to win this marathon," he said with a voice filled with worry.

Christian smirked at Augustin as he saw him being weighed down by the cause he decided to set for himself and now defend. He opened his mouth to say something, but changed his mind. He did not want to spoil the fun before it began. Indeed, Christian was only there for the unusual experience. He was not going to get in the way of his own entertainment during these hundred hours.

Not far from them, the organizers' assistant was excitedly and proudly standing by the door, holding the list of male competitors.

"Get ready to join your partners!" he ordered. "Line up in numerical order!"

As the numbers of the male participants were being called, so were the numbers of the women's section. The competitors were coming out, meeting their partner in the middle of the dance floor, and gradually forming blissful couples. The First Lady and the entire audience erupted in exciting applause.

Dressed with a simple blouse and a flared out skirt her mother had sewn for her for the occasion, Emilia smiled shily and blushingly. She trembled a little when her brother took her hand. She felt unsure of herself now and doubted she would be standing at the very end. And certainly, she could not see how she would be able to compete against a seemingly strong opponent like Adrienne Dolan.

During the time she just spent with the other young women, Emilia noticed Adrienne Dolan's kindness, but also her haughty side. From a conversation she overheard, she discovered that Adrienne Dolan was not a young girl. She was a young widow. And now, she chose to leave her only child for four days in the care of an aunt in order to compete, determined to bring home the 5,000 *gourdes*.

"I'm scared!" Emilia confessed to her brother while glancing around.

"Don't worry. We're going to win," Emilio said reassuringly while squeezing her hand. "Dad trained us too well. No one else but us can win the prize."

Emilio offered freely these kind words but he, too, felt doubtful about their chances to win the competition. He looked at the faces of all the strangers clapping for them. Then, he took a deep breath and raised his chin haughtily.

As the participants gathered finally on the dance floor, the musicians of the *Orchestre Caraïbes*, all wearing the same colorful outfits, readied themselves with their instruments.

Dr. Wallon remained near Mrs. Estimé as the organizers stood in front of the orchestra. Then, Mr. Gomez took the microphone and flashed a broad smile.

"Her Excellency, Madam First Lady, dignitaries, ladies, and gentlemen: Welcome to this grand event, the likes of which you have never seen in Haiti! Welcome to the 100 Hour Grand Resistance Dance Marathon!"

A deluge of applause welcomed Mr. Gomez's introduction. The ovations were so loud that the First Lady, amazed, looked around the room.

Taking turns, Mr. Gomez and Mr. Carrey informed the audience of the marathon's rules, which, purposely, were visible everywhere on the trees.

"We're going to experience some thrilling hours that we won't soon forget!" exclaimed Mr. Gomez.

"Absolutely," Mr. Carrey added. "To allow participants to stay in the race, each couple will be entitled to a five-minute rest after each hour of dancing. However, they can accumulate the rest minutes over two, three, four, five, or six hours. Thus, a couple who has danced for example, six consecutive hours without a rest will be entitled to thirty consecutive minutes of rest, and so on."

The rules caused a few to mumble in the crowd. Many spectators saw themselves unable to dance for so many hours.

"The person wearing the number attached to their clothing is the main dancer," Mr. Gomez informed. "This dancer can change partners as many times as he or she wishes. If the dancer manages to complete 100 hours of dancing, he or she will become the winner of $1,000 USD, which is equivalent to 5,000 *gourdes* in Haitian currency."

The crowd's attention was now turned to the competitors. They were fascinated by the participation of women in such a contest. Some conservative factions were shocked and alarmed by their presence. But young people were especially captivated by strong women like Adrienne Dolan.

"I'm sure she'll win," said one female spectator.

"Women don't have as much stamina as men," her seemingly fiancé replied. "In two or three hours, it'll be the end for all of them."

"Where did that stupid idea come from?" the young woman asked, both amused and surprised.

"Stupid?... Okay. You'll see."

Not far from this crowd, the travel-and-leisure journalists were constantly taking notes and photos, occasionally questioning Mr. Montrose and his assistant to ensure they understood certain words or phrases.

"If no dancers manage to beat the 100-hour requirement," Mr. Gomez continued, "the $1,000 USD prize will be divided proportionally among the three finalists who will come the closest to 100 hours. And if two or more dancers manage to beat the set record of 100 hours of non-stop dancing, the tournament will continue and the $1,000 USD prize will be awarded to the dancer with the most endurance."

"The Organizing Committee will be the ultimate judge," Mr. Carrey explained. "We will meticulously record the hours of dancing and the minutes of rest for each participant. We will eliminate dancers who spontaneously withdraw due to fatigue and may, at the same time, disqualify those who do not follow the rules."

Among the competitors, Joseph Morose had a hard time identifying his own son. He wanted to show him off to the journalists. Timidly, he rose slightly from his seat to better point him out, but he realized that the participants were already pairing up.

Yet, Augustin and Christian were positioned in the middle of the floor, their partners barely paying attention to the rules. While Jocelyn was due to arrive later in the evening, Mireille and Agathe seemed eager to begin a job for which they were about to be paid more than three time the minimum daily wage set at 1.50 *gourdes* ($0.30 USD).

Meanwhile, far behind them, dressed in a traditional outfit, Shilette was flashing a bizarre smile. Her lips were almost trembling. She no longer had that relaxed look. She was glancing furtively from side to side.

"What's wrong with you?" Solon asked her.

Shilette took a while to respond, struggling to find the right words. If the First Lady's presence intimidated her, the recounting of the rules finally made her realize the magnitude of the challenge she was about to undertake.

"I've never danced in front of so many people before," she whispered. "And besides, I don't know how to dance at all."

Solon became pale. Not once he had the impression that Shilette did not know how to dance. Rosa never mentioned that fact when they were discussing their agreement. If it's true that they should have practice, he never had the slight doubt that such a beautiful woman could not dance. A cold sweat trickled down his spine. He was afraid that Shilette was about to let him down.

"You don't need to know how to dance. Don't look at these people. You're a hibiscus flower that will soon bloom on this stage... Follow me. That's all I ask. Don't stop moving. Don't stop...," he begged while grabbing the young girl's hands.

The sounds of a few trumpets accompanied by a slow, subtle drum roll put an end to Solon's pleas. The couples took their places, looking into each other's eyes, each trying to support one another with a trembling smile. Then suddenly, trumpets, cymbals, cha-cha, the entire ensemble of the *Orchestre Caraïbes* kicked-of the competition with a harmonious resounding music.

The *méringue* music suddenly filled the club, spilled over into the surrounding streets, and echoed over the calm sea. Solon and Shilette, Emilio and Emilia, Christian and Mireille, Augustin and Agathe, and the rest of the participants joined into the movement of the music under the encouragement of the audience.

Clifford F. Mayer, number 60, was, from the start, in direct competition with Constantin, number 10. Both young men simultaneously sought to be in front of the First Lady and the officials accompanying her. Both wanted to be seen and, above all, to command attention with their charismatic personalities. Discovering Constantin's maneuver, Mayer continued to dance confidently, trying every means to stand out with his mastery of the *méringue.*

Solon Férila, number 95, was observing this silent battle without feeling the slightest fear. A kind of bravery was animating him, instilling great confidence. All the plans he had been mulling over for days were finally being materialized before him. Mayer with all his experiences was just an unworthy competitor. Solon's dreams were bigger than all of them combined.

Solon looked at Shilette with a decided gaze of determination. He greeted the young girl with an imaginary hat, puffed out his chest, squared his shoulders, then, placing one hand behind his back, he extended the other to her. The drumbeat just brought back memories of folk festivals and seeing his father drumming at the very instrument.

"Gentlemen get ready to dance! Look at your ladies in the eyes! Turn your ladies in place! Gentlemen, hold on to your ladies! Cross the figure eight!" Solon heard his father's voice commanded.

Shilette recognized the movements; it was similar to a folk dance in *Cayes-Jacmel*. Little by little, the memories of her childhood revived her, instilled in her the confidence she needed. Shilette lifted a hem of her *'karabela'* dress (Haitian folk dress lined with a generous white-laced underskirt). She placed her two fists first on her swinging hips. She got closer to Solon, her feet pointing to either side, her hoop earrings fluttering in all directions, her steps timed, in perfect sync with Solon's.

Despite the number of competitors on the dance floor, the spectacle Solon and Shilette were putting on did not escaped the crowd who shouted their admiration. Rosa was surprised by the audience's reaction, happy to see her daughter's shyness vanished, and giving herself entirely over to the sound of the drum.

Solon's big movements amused Emilio Cantave. Identified as number 18, he was barely moving, holding his sister by the waist. His heart beat returned to normal from the previous excitement. Emilia, intently concentrating on her steps, was resting both hands on her brother's shoulders. From the beginning of the contest, the twins mentally noted a sequence of errors made by the other participants, almost mocking the burst of energy some displayed. But they did not let themselves be distracted. They studied every gesture, every movement they needed to make. They knew they had a hundred hours ahead of them. They had to preserve their energy if they wanted to complete the mission entrusted to them. As they continued to move, Emilia's face suddenly relaxed.

"Look!" she shouted. "Alfred and Béatrice are here!"

Surprised, Emilio turned to his left. While he expected to see Alfred, who supported his participation from the start, Béatrice's presence came as a bit of a shock.

"Go ahead, Milo! Go, Mila!" Alfred shouted from the excited crowd.

Emilio smiled mischievously, realizing that the incessant publicity both on the radio and in the newspapers, had finally piqued his sister's curiosity.

Indeed, with her coworkers desperate to watch the competition, Béatrice was becoming increasingly embarrassed to deny that members of her family were participating. The enthusiasm for the marathon also helped her to discover the societal classes interested in it, thus seeing an opportunity to exploit.

Consequently, on the evening of the launch, she wore a navy-blue dress with small white polka dots, color matching gloves, handbag, and shoes. Béatrice came to the *Bord-de-Mer* with a simple mission: she did not want to be just another woman in the crowd. She wanted to stand out and attract the attention of someone who would help her achieve her ultimate dream of immigrating to Paris. She was convinced that settling down forever in the City of Lights was the solution to the monotony of the retail career that was laying ahead of her.

The crowded venue made no impression on Béatrice. Realizing that she and Alfred were too far away from the First Lady and the other dignitaries, she thought of moving closer to the dance floor. Cleverly, she found a way to get to the front of the line to be admired. She did not want to scream like her brother. Her silence, her way of clapping, her elegance, her entire being should be a testament to her dearest desire.

The calculated maneuvers finally caught the attention of one of the travel-and-leisure journalists. Béatrice exuded such mystery that he could not help but stare at her in the middle of the crowd. After several long minutes, their eyes met. And as if this intrigued look sent an audible message to her ears, Béatrice raised her head slightly to look at him. She mentally cleared the area around her, seeing only the journalist who was quickly reloading his camera wanting not to lose this unique moment. Standing in the background of the dancers, surrounded by the effervescent crowd, she let herself be photographed. She smiled at the corners of her lips, highlighted with a bright red lipstick. Her message was finally passed on.

While dancing, Christian Grégoire, number 30, found himself near Béatrice's brother. Alfred's shouts and all those who supported Emilio caused a pang in his heart. Beside a work colleague whom he noticed entering the room, he had not seen anyone else who came to see him. Yet, in the days following the announcement of his participation for a worthy cause, his mother softened a little, his sisters were full of praise for him, even his father advised him on what type of shoes to wear. Up till now, nothing pointed to this disinterest.

On his part, Augustin Montrose, number 31, was also hoping to see his father. As soon as he entered the dance floor, he scanned the room in all directions. His father must have been held once again by his professional obligations.

He felt dejected for having shared his deepest feelings; feelings he felt were dismissed by his father's absence.

However, after many attempts, Joseph Montrose and his assistant finally spotted his son among the dancers.

"There he is!" Abel shouted excitedly. "Go, Mr. Augustin! Go!"

Mr. Montrose jumped up from his chair, eyes full of pride. How he would have loved for the entire crowd to know his son's genuine heart and the reason for his participation!

"Here's my son!" he indicated to one of the journalists.

"The one in the khaki jacket?" the journalist questioned.

"Yes! That's him! Go, Augustin!"

The familiar voice slipped through the commotion and reached Augustin like a gust of fresh air. The young man's heart leaped. He breathed deeply; his eyes were wide open, happy to emerge from anonymity.

Augustin did a turn that positioned him in the direction of the person who shouted his name.

"Go on, Mr. Augustin! Go, Mr. Christian!"

"Go, Christian and Augustin! Go, my son!"

Augustin followed the voice to the island-turned-restaurant, tapping Christian's shoulder repeatedly, as if he had just witnessed an unexpected miracle.

"They're here!" he shouted. "My father is here!"

This presence invigorated the young man and his friend. Every step Augustin took became like a hymn to the patients of the sanatorium. Seeing his father was the ultimate proof that he understood and supported him in his quest for happiness.

Mireille and Agathe sensed the change in Christian and Augustin's attitude. They were moving with more enthusiasm. These young ladies from a folk group mastered the dance techniques. They knew how to let the music sway and move them; their gestures became lively, agile, and supple, and transformed their steps into a show.

Thus, the dancing couples carved the dance floor into rhythmic images. Their focused allowed them to perfectly execute their planned choreography, revealing their unique and diverse styles. At times, this haphazard mix of dancers resembled a collective. Some couples were talking to each other while others were laughing heartily. From time to time, men stepped aside to twirl their partners, which made the crowd roar with joy. Some participants were emerging as favorites and speculations about who would win went rampant among the audience.

"Number 60 is so elegant!" said a young woman to two others accompanying her. "Look how he holds his partner. It's as if she's just floating."

"Too light for my taste," replied the other. "Look at number 48 instead. He makes her move with such vigor!"

"Anyway," emphasized the third, "my favorite is number 5. I like his originality. He and numbers 30 and 31 are definitely real dancers."

Suddenly, the young woman fell silent, letting out a cry of astonishment. Two couples collided and the audience held their breath in anticipation of what was going to happen next.

"My God!" the young spectator said.

Solon just shoved Augustin so hard that he staggered. The audience stared intently on the two men. Frightened, Shilette put her hand over her mouth while Solon apologized endlessly, understanding finally he was not alone on the dance floor. In their fervor, Shilette and Solon momentarily disrupted the natural directional flow of the rest of the dancers.

With the sheer number of dancers, it was expected that something like that would be inevitable. In fact,

Augustin recognized from the start that extravagant improvisations were to be avoided. Christian and he were forced to restrain their movement and that irritated them. Deep down, he wanted to dance freely like Solon.

Augustin smiled and made a gesture to reassure the young man, which calmed down part of the crowd who were expecting an argument. Quickly forgetting what had happened, the onlookers resumed their shouts of encouragement. The excitement of the first hours of the marathon washed out mistakes and united in a euphoric craze.

CHAPTER 7
And Twenty-Four hours elapsed

While the competition started at the *Bord-de-Mer,* Marie-Cécile and her parents were slowly climbing the steps of the *Rex Theatre* in the *Champ de Mars* entertainment district. The luminous letters of the marquee of the theatre were reflecting on the young girl's yellow dress. Her decided steps were testifying to her impatience to attend this last performance of her older sister before her departure for Austria.

When the Grégoire family entered the theater, the lobby and its grand staircase were already filled with people who came to support Marie-Agnès.

"Lynn!" exclaimed Mrs. Grégoire enthusiastically. "What are you doing here? I thought you were on tour with the singers of La Scala of Milan?"

"No. It will be next week."

"Honestly, you seemed tireless! You'll have to teach me your secret for maintaining that perfect complexion despite fatigue."

Along with her two daughters, Lynn Volmar was flanked by her husband. The skin tone of the latter alluded to his Spanish ancestry was passed on to his daughters. All smiles, the women kissed each other on the cheek while the men, dressed in business attire, exchanged a warm handshake. As always, their conversation eventually turned into a business meeting. Guy Volmar who was the principal of one of the few private schools in the capital, wanted to share his desire to offer financial literacy classes to the graduating seniors. Roger Grégoire thought the idea was excellent and agreed with his friend on the day and time they could put up together a curriculum.

Mrs. Grégoire looked at the two men before exchanging a knowing nod with Mrs. Volmar.

"Anyway," she said, "thank you for coming for Marie-Agnès!"

"Elsa, you know we never miss any of your daughters' concerts," replied Guy Volmar.

With a puzzled face, Mrs. Volmar looked at all corners of the lobby for someone.

"Where is Christian?" she asked.

Mrs. Grégoire fluttered her eyelashes and flashed a deep sentiment of pride.

"My dear, he followed your advice. For the past twenty-four hours now, he's been participating in the dance marathon," she retorqued.

"The money Augustin and he will win," Marie-Cécile quickly informed the Volmars, "will be donated to the Sanatorium of Port-au-Prince."

"Really?" Gisèle Volmar asked, her eyes sparkling with interest. "Augustin will do that for them?"

"What a generous soul! You have a wonderful son, my dear!" exclaimed Mrs. Volmar.

"You know," said Mr. Volmar, "this marathon is a real success. Right now, it's one of the most popular attractions at the *Bord-de-Mer* (waterfront area)."

"I'm really happy that I was able to help the organizers get the green light from the Department of Tourism," added his wife. "We couldn't attend the start of the competition. But tonight, after the concert, we plan to go see for ourselves. Were you there for the launch?"

Although Elsa Grégoire saw in her son's participation a way to showcase her family's philanthropic beliefs, she felt no reason to be seen in a walkathon. She simply could not imagine her husband and herself in a crowd of people of uncertain lineage, shouting out the numbers of their favorite dancers.

"We had too much to do," she hastened to reply.

Marie-Cécile stared at her mother, perplexed, searching her mind desperately for the "too much" that filled her mother's idle days and prevented her from supporting Christian. The young girl let out a small sigh. She would have so loved to see this contest the newspapers were constantly talking about! Her heart filled with pride as she imagined the elegance of her brother and Augustin on the dance floor.

"If it's okay with you and if she's interested, Marie-Cécile can come with us," said Mrs. Volmar who noticed the young girl's distressed expression.

Marie-Cécile immediately turned her head toward her parents, her eyes shining with excitement, silently begging for their approval.

The direct invitation made Mrs. Grégoire somewhat embarrassed, as she could not imagine her daughter attending this walkathon either. However, while the fear of gossips made her unenthusiastic, her longtime friendship with Lynn Volmar prevented her from refusing.

"Why not?" she replied half-heartedly.

Gisèle, Violette, and Marie-Cécile exchanged a knowing smile. An excitement was boiling inside of them.

"The theatre must be almost full," Mr. Grégoire intervened, seeing a few waiting at the entrance hall. "We have to find our seats."

The small group took the grand staircase, which opened onto a spacious mezzanine. The house was almost full of spectators letting out whispers, leafing through the evening's program.

"Good evening," said one of the ushers to the group.

"Good evening," replied Mr. Grégoire while showing his invitation. "Our seats are reserved."

The usher took the invitations, briefly examined them, and put up a pleasant smile.

"Please follow me. Your seats are at the front."

Covered with a red carpet that sloped down toward the stage, the floor and the central aisles were lit by small lamps placed on the back of the seats. This subtle lighting served as a runway for Mrs. Grégoire, who walked with queenly steps while discreetly greeting a few acquaintances who were admiring them.

Once they arrived at their seats, Roger Grégoire and Guy Volmar politely stepped aside to let their daughters and wives pass and sat comfortably in the red armchairs facing the immense stage. Marie-Cécile was fascinated by the vaulted ceiling with its sparkling chandeliers reflecting the light from the artistically decorated paneling and the discreet sconces on the walls. She raised her head to admire the grandeur of the place and the refined choice of the *Rex Théâtre* ivory and gold interior design.

On the balcony, which overlooked part of the auditorium, she saw Miss Dreyfus, dressed in black as usual, sitting stiff like a statue. The young girl waved at her before turning her focus on the stage.

"The evening promises to be fantastic!" Gisèle exclaimed in her thin voice as she looked at the program her sister was holding.

"Justin Elie, Ludovic Lamothe, Edmond Saintongue, Carmen Brouard… all the best masters of Haitian classical music," added Violette in a floral dress.

The lights dimmed and the whispers in the room died down. The curtain rose and revealed the modish orchestra. A cellist gave the tunning note, leading the other musicians with their instruments, creating a small cacophony. As the conductor entered the stage with his baton, the musicians all rose at once, watching him stepping onto his platform. The audience greeted him with applause when he bowed. A few seconds later, Marie-Agnès made her entrance. Her shiny dark brown hair was perfectly pulled back. She was wearing a long, lavender gala gown that exposed her shoulders and complemented her tanned complexion.

"If she has worn the red dress I recommended, your sister would have looked even more stunning tonight," Mrs. Grégoire whispered to Marie-Cécile.

Marie-Cécile pressed her lips a little, annoyed by her mother's insistence on controlling everything.

"This one suits her perfectly, mom. Otherwise, the color would have been an unfortunate match with the armchairs."

Marie-Agnès gracefully bowed to the audience before sitting in front of the grand piano. The conductor raised his baton, waiting for the signal. Spotlights fell on the pianist, who first closed her eyes. Her fingers brushing the keys, she started very softly. Then crescendo, her slightly detached yet connected way of playing the notes gave life to the first musical bar of Edmond Saintonge's *Élégie*.

Marie-Agnès was playing with nuance and subtleness, her body bending along with her hands' movements, allowing herself to be transformed, revealing feelings that only music could draw from the depths of her being. The house acoustics was so clear that each musical phrasing united the audience with the pianist's emotions. The strings were blending in perfect harmony with brass, percussions and woodwind instruments. From Ludovic Lamothe's *Feuillet no. 1* to the infinite ranges of Justin Elie's *Chant de la Montagne*, all the mastery of Marie-Agnès's art was exteriorized, leaving the entire room vibrating with emotion.

The concert ended with a deluge of applause. Marie-Agnès stood up graciously as the conductor took her by the hand and led her to the front of the stage to be admired. The spectators approached quickly from all of the auditorium to throw roses at their feet.

The young lady looked up toward the balcony and gave Miss Dreyfus a kiss of thanks. The piano teacher reunited both hands in front of her mouth as tears rolled down on her cheeks. All around her, the most snobbish patrons seating in the lodges, on the two balconies, and the entire house rose up and fervently applauded the pianist, the conductor, and the orchestra. A chosen little girl came up on the stage and brought to Marie-Agnès a wreath of flowers that she could barely hold in her tiny, child arms.

Although she was not expecting it this time, Marie-Agnès had no trouble recognizing where this oversized bouquet came from. At every concert, it was always Augustin who sent flowers, and this time, despite his absence, he did not forget. Marie-Agnès closed her eyes and smelled the bouquet, envisioning, for a fleeting moment, Augustin beside her. All the praises she was receiving were also for him; they were for his anticipated great achievement in behalf of the Sanatorium of Port-au-Prince. Marie-Agnès blinked, trying to collect herself, smiling stupidly at her family, friends, and at the entire audience who were acclaiming her.

Moved, Mrs. Grégoire was clinging to her husband's arm, wiping away a tear, realizing that, the sacrifices they made over the years were worth it. Elsa Grégoire recalled how World War II also affected the country's wealthy families. Very few of them were still able to afford the services of a piano teacher. To relieve the stress of expenses, she and her husband had to cut back on outings and the many private receptions they used to organize; they rationed everything they could to help their daughter achieve her dream of becoming a professional pianist…

Pressed by many parties, the Grégoire family could hardly leave the theater. They were being stopped every step of the way. When they finally left the *Rex Théâtre,* Gisèle, Violette, and Marie-Cécile hurried to stand by Mr. Volmar's Ford while their parents exchanged final greetings.

"We have to wait for Marie-Agnès," said Mrs. Grégoire. "Would you kindly bring Marie-Cécile home?"

"Certainly. Let's say around 11:00 p.m.?" suggested Mrs. Volmar.

"Sure. I know my daughter is in good hands."

Mr. Grégoire went to the car, took a few bills out of his wallet, and gave them to his daughter.

"In case you need something… Remember that to buy things at the pavilions, you'll need tickets. So, talk to Mr. Volmar first. He'll guide you."

"Every time I go there", Mr. Volmar interjected, "I forget that detail… But Roger, why did the Department of Finance adopt this procedure?"

"It's to facilitate the mercantile operations at the exhibition site. A way for the Central Bank to better manage the flow of cash."

Puzzled, Mr. Volmar raised his eyebrows, thinking that this system was a little complicated.

"Any way, if there's one thing the Central Bank has done that deserves applause, it's putting an end to these checks that anyone could endorse in behalf of 'friends'."

"Exactly," said Mr. Grégoire. "A real mess that needed to be fixed."

"All right, all right!" intervened Mrs. Grégoire. "Enough business talk! You're both terrible!"

"Enjoy the rest of your evening Elsa, my dear," said Mrs. Volmar while exchanging a goodbye kiss on the cheek with her friend. "You'll congratulate Marie-Agnès once again on her impeccable performance."

The drive from *Champ de Mars* to the *Cité de l'Exposition* was not long. If he took *St. Honoré* Street, Mr. Volmar could have easily continued to *Oswald Durand* Street, which would have taken them to the South Gate, one of the two entrances that allowed cars to pass through. But it was 9:30 p.m., and the city was still alive; pedestrians and cars were eagerly heading toward the *Bord-de-Mer*. So, Mr. Volmar wanted to show the city to his daughters and Marie-Cécile before arriving at the *Palmistes*.

Guy Volmar first headed down *Lalue* neighborhood, took *Des Miracles* Street, then *Du Quai* Street before turning towards the City Hall and reaching the North Gate. This was where the sixteen pavilions of the participating countries began.

The moon, in the clear and starry sky, was reflecting on the sea like a sparkling disc partaking in the city's festivities. Several people were standing on the waterfront, breathing in the sea air. They were gazing at the hundreds of small yellow, red, green, blue, and orange light bulbs that were lining from the wharf, behind the Customs House, to the district of *Martissant* in the distance. Facing the Caribbean Sea, buildings of all shapes and sizes were visibly illuminated from the inside as well as the outside facades. The Post Office and the Tourism Pavilions were also reflecting a grandiose appearance.

"How beautiful!" Marie-Cécile blurted out, pressing her face against the car window.

Despite this detour, which made her even more impatient, the young girl wanted to see what the exhibition site looked like at night. Indeed, when she came with her family to dine at the *Carillon* or shop at *La Belle Créole*, it was always in broad daylight, when *Morne l'Hôpital*, with its deep green slopes, unfolded, serving as a backdrop to this city over the ocean. Marie-Cécile never seen the stores, the restaurants, and the clubs' neon signs illuminating the streets.

Mr. Volmar drove to Harry Truman Boulevard and then parked the car almost in front of *Quai Colomb*. A luxury yacht setting sail in this port attracted as much attention as the large statue mounted on an enormous pedestal.

"Who's that?" asked Marie-Cécile, pointing at the statue.

"Christopher Columbus," replied Violette.

Intrigued, Marie-Cécile stared at the impressive representation of the Spanish conqueror half-kneeling, holding a cross in one hand and touching his barely drawn sword with the other. She was interested by the symbolism of the gesture that conveyed both submission and authority.

"Strange posture..."

Mr. Volmar pouted his lips in disdain.

"Not so much," he corrected. "It's exactly the posture of someone asking forgiveness for all the crimes he has committed in the name of religion..."

The Volmar girls and Marie-Cécile remained silent, taken by surprise by the depth of Mr. Volmar's words.

"Guy, come on! What are you telling the children?" his wife interjected, understanding their dismay.

Mr. Volmar straightened up, his brows furrowing, his face marked by sadness and indignation.

"What do you mean by what am I telling them? It wasn't old age that killed the island's first inhabitants. It was the disease brought by those conquerors. It was forced labor, slavery to which the natives were subjected. A real genocide that took them all away..."

"Okay. Calm down, my friend," Mrs. Volmar commanded. "This evening is supposed to be a relaxing night with our children. And now you're turning it into a lecture."

"You have such passion for history, Dad," Gisèle added cheerfully, trying to calm her father down.

Mr. Volmar and his passengers stepped out of the car and were walking, feeling the light night breeze on their skin.

"Well, if telling the truth is passion, then so be it! I hope, my dear daughter, that you will have as much passion when you pursue your medical studies. This country desperately needs it!"

Gisèle smiled, clinging to Mr. Volmar's arms.

"Of course, my dear Papa," she said, her voice filled with admiration for her father's unwavering sense of justice.

Marie-Cécile's eyes gleamed, giving way to a small smile at the corners of her lips that betrayed a slight envy for the Volmars' freedom of thought. This desire to be like them, which she barely managed to hide, was nevertheless noticed by Mrs. Volmar.

Having grown up and having run around in the same circle of youngsters as Elsa Grégoire, Lynn Volmar was well aware of her friend's old-fashioned ideas. How many times has she confronted her regarding her convictions; chief among them was this: any self-respecting young woman should marry a rich man who would take care of her for the rest of her life without having to damage her nails...

Mrs. Volmar smiled as she clutched Marie-Cécile's arms; she wanted the latter to know she understood her. She felt a strong desire to help the young girl find meaning in her life. Times were changing and the Haitian society was now offering a whole range of opportunities for women in their professional lives. The creation of the school *Lycée des Jeunes Filles* recently began this revolution, opening doors to higher education that previously seemed an inaccessible path for young girls.

Lynn Volmar took a deep breath. Just as she encouraged her daughters to embrace these changes, she would make it her mission to help Marie-Cécile understand that she, too, could now make her own choice.

Violette freed Marie-Cécile from her mother's grasp, almost pushing her toward a gigantic illuminated fountain. Between the pavilions of Guatemala, Italy, the United States, Cuba, and Mexico, the fountain was a place for families to relax, a playground for a few children, and a meeting place for lovers among the flowering oleanders and hibiscuses.

"It's even more beautiful at night!" exclaimed Violette, marveling at the fountain.

The illuminated fountain was a sequence of circular pools supporting a circle of graceful women. Streams of water shot in illuminated and multicolored jets; they rose and fell to the rhythm of classical music. The main water jet, which was following the final notes of a Beethoven symphony, collapsed and splashed Marie-Cécile. The Volmar girls skipped away while laughing heartily. Mr. and Mrs. Volmar also laughed at their childish reaction.

On the way back to the car, Marie-Cécile notice monumental statues that were installed everywhere, between bushes, behind oleanders, or simply in the middle of a garden.

"Where do they come from?"

"It's an outdoor exhibition," replied Mrs. Volmar. "There are exactly thirty-two of them, some are made of marble and others of bronze."

"The artists who created them are truly talented," said Gisèle. "Do you know them, Mom?"

"No. In fact, they were loaned to the Haitian government by the Metropolitan Museum of New York."

"Just for the duration of the exhibition?" asked Violette.

"No. A renewable contract was signed for 99 years, provided the government takes care of them, of course."

Amazed by the artistry, Marie-Cécile and her friends approached one of the statues to admire it more closely. Their fingers traced their shapes, glided over the smooth material, and felt the softness of the marble. It was the first time they were seeing a life-size sculpture of a human body.

The small group walked for a few more minutes. Then they got back in the car and sped to the roundabout where the Arch of the Exhibition stood, illuminated by spotlights. Apart from official vehicles, no other vehicles were allowed in the *Palmistes* area. So, Mr. Volmar and his passengers got out of the Ford and walked the rest of the way to the club. The eclectic appearance of people on the streets pointed to where they were coming from. Some were in suits or evening wear; and still others were in tropical outfits, testifying to the diversity and richness of the exhibition's offerings.

Barely audible at first, the music coming from the club became increasingly distinct. A line of people, hardly deterred by the 1 *gourde* ($0.20 USD) admission fee, was standing in front of the door when the Volmars and Marie-Agnès finally arrived. Hundreds of curious spectators, both tourists and locals, were filling through the palm trees, eager to see who could resist three more days and nights of non-stop dancing.

Despite the crowd, Mrs. Volmar spotted one of the organizers. He was whispering a few words into a musician's ear.

"Gomez is on this side," she told her husband.

Lynn Volmar grabbed her husband's arm as she followed him in the direction of Mr. Gomez. Gisèle, Violette, and Marie-Cécile quickened the pace, holding hands, afraid to lose each other. Marie-Cécile struggled to make her way through the fans. Though, unaccustomed to such a large crowd, she was enjoying the festive atmosphere, feeling as excited as the crowd.

About fifty dancers were dancing on the tune of a *bolero*. The intricacies of the dance separated the skilled couples from the novices. Some still seemed to be alert and others were already dragging their bodies.

Dr. Wallon was vigilantly scanning the dancers to detect anyone with a slight inclination of giving up. For some time now, he has been particularly focused on a dancer: Constantin, number 10.

"You're extremely fatigue," the doctor repeated for the umpteenth time.

"I just need a pick-me-up, doctor," Constantin protested miserably, his eyes barely open.

"I can't give you any more vitamins! Stop immediately!" the doctor ordered.

"A little punch made with beaten eggs and rhum sprinkled with nutmeg will do just fine, doctor," the young man rambled.

Clifford F. Mayer let out loud an insolent laugh. Solon raised his eyebrows in indignation. While it was true that Constantin's impulsiveness irritated him at first, he discovered that the young man was good-natured and pleasant. With his camp bed set up next to Emilio's, Constantin did not hesitate to share his surplus of supplies. It was thanks to him that on several occasions sleep did not overpower them, thus saving them from elimination.

The insistence of Constantin and of his equally broken partner commanded pity. Emilia reflected on the situation. She remembered meeting this Constantin on the first day. Although she interacted just a little with him thereafter, Emilio shared his jokes, recounted his gestures of solidarity.

"We have to help him!" the young woman begged.

"But there's nothing we can do," Emilio realized sadly. "Otherwise, we'll be the ones eliminated."

With a concerned face, Dr. Wallon hurried past Emilio and headed toward the organizers.

"Number 10 must leave the floor immediately! They're both in severe asthenia!"

"Very well, Doctor," replied Mr. Carrey as he pointed the couple to his assistants.

"Ladies and gentlemen," Mr. Gomez said. "We must announce the elimination of number 10 and his companion."

"Oh!" the spectators let out unanimously in disappointment.

The organizers' assistants escorted Constantin and his partner off the dance floor. This removal prompted two other completely exhausted couples to abandon the marathon.

Marie-Cécile followed Constantin with worried eyes as he walked with bowed head. His departure frightened the young girl, who just realized what fatigue could cause. She looked for her brother and Augustin, wondering if they already ate; if they were thirsty; if they had enough rest; if, like the eliminated couple, they were dancing their last minutes.

"But where are they?" she asked standing on tiptoe as she scanned the room.

"There they are!" shouted Gisèle.

Augustin and Mireille were standing behind Christian and Jocelyn. With Mr. Gomez's help, the Volmars and Marie-Cécile came closer to the dance floor. Marie-Cécile gestured wildly, attracting her brother's attention. Christian and Augustin responded with the same enthusiastic gesture as they carried on with their supple and fluid movements.

"They're the best!" stated Marie-Cécile, both excited and relieved.

Happy to share the dance floor with fewer dancers, Christian was freely improvising which made his sister and the Volmar girls burst out laughing.

"He's even more handsome when he dances," Gisèle whispered in Marie-Cécile's ear.

"Yes, I know. Christian is a fine dancer…"

"I'm talking about Augustin," Gisèle corrected. "Don't you think so? Oh my! He makes my heart race!"

Surprised, Marie-Cécile stared at her friend. She was not expecting such revelation. She looked in the direction of the young man whom unspoken secret she knew: he was deeply in love with her sister. Marie-Cécile fought the urge to let out a mocking laugh. She did not see how Gisèle could have even a slight chance. But she remained silent and simply smiled.

Augustin, indeed, stood out by his style of dancing. With Jocelyn's arrival at the eighth hour, he and Christian were able to switch partners. The young man was now dancing with Mireille, who was putting to good use the learned steps the current music was suggesting. Precise in every one of them, she was smiling while looking at Augustin straight in the eyes. This eye contact seemed to liven up Augustin's determination who wanted to send at that very moment a message to all and, certainly, to Marie-Agnès. With his steps, Augustin confirmed his resoluteness to win; they affirmed his desire to lay the check at Marie-Agnès' feet and prove that he was not a fool.

The languorous melodies of the *bolero* stopped abruptly. The sound of trumpets, cymbals, cha-chas, and drums rose suddenly into the air with such force that all tired legs woke up! The audience embraced the change of music; the spectators let themselves be swept away by the whirlwind of the rhythms of a *méringue*! Gisèle, Violette, and Marie-Cécile danced, shouting joyfully in a manner unbefitting young ladies of their social status.

Although surprised, Mrs. Volmar had a smirk on her face; she was happy to see her daughters and Marie-Cécile loosening up while supporting Christian and Augustin.

Despite the noise, the two commentators from Radio 4VRW did their best to broadcast live the latest news.

"We're still in Les *Palmistes*! It's been more than 25 hours since the couples started dancing! Sadly, numbers 10, 17, and 21 have just been eliminated! We are witnessing the first hours of this sensational competition! Simply extraordinary, dear listeners!"

"Yes, EXTRAORDINARY is the right word! More than 5,000 spectators have already witnessed those 25 hours! The atmosphere is one of laughter, joy, and emotion! A consuming fire that only victory can extinguish has gripped the competitors gathered under the *Palmistes*! Come live this event with us and behold with your own eyes this incredible marathon!"

CHAPTER 8
Then Forty hours…

Hours later, while the festivities at the *Palmistes* area was in full rhythmic swing, Cherilus left the crowd to return home in *La Saline*. The strong smell of the sea was attracting birds looking for small fish to feast on. Despite their shrill cries, Cherilus did not hear them, nor did he see the tourists disembarking from their yachts or those rushing to help them carry their belongings in exchange for a few coins. He was walking slowly, unaffected by the bustle at *Quai Colomb*, as if he was alone in the entire world.

As the competition reached its fortieth hours mark early that afternoon, Cherilus was thrown into a retrospection. In the beginning Solon desires were just an unattainable joke; but his tenacity opened Cherilus' eyes to the possibility of him winning. It's been over two days since his friend was toiling on a dance floor in a contest that attracted the nation's elite.

Cherilus vividly remembered the advice he gave Solon when he was living in the town of *Jérémie*. How prophetic! He encouraged him to seek a new life in Port-au-Prince, the city of dreams. Indeed, the capital was the seat of political and commercial power, and higher education; it was the city of future princes. Facing Solon's doubts, he offered his house as a trampling for his dreams if he ever decided to abandon the fields that now lie fallow unwillingly.

Solon finally did muster up his courage. At nineteen, he simply said goodbye to *Grande-Anse*. Leaving everything behind, focused on a better future, he booked a passage on a boat from the city of *Jérémie*, destination Port-au-Prince. He traveled an entire night, sat among animals, different type of goods, and pressed up against seasick people who did not hold back emptying the content of their stomach. He arrived in Port-au-Prince the next morning. He felt an uneasiness but a certain wonder took hold of him. All these strangers, these architects, these engineers, these workers, these large machines coming and going, transported him far from the peaceful rural life he was accustomed to. Though Cherilus previously prepared him for this arrival, everything paled in comparison to the scale of the operations he was witnessing at the wharf.

Despite his fear, Solon began to walk straight ahead with a bag containing all his belongings under his arm. He stopped in front different groups of workers as he walked, hoping to see Cherilus among them. Finally, as his confidence began to turn into distress, he ran into Cherilus, casually taking a break somewhere along Harry Truman Boulevard. Among so many workers, this encounter was perceived as a divine intervention…

Exhausted by his long journey, Cherilus entered his humble house and collapsed onto a straw chair, forgetting to greet his wife. His heavy legs, aching feet, left him unresponsive to the affectionate gestures of his children. They were clinging to his pants and smiling with happiness. After a little while, Cherilus finally paid attention to his pregnant wife, who, despite their poverty, still retained all her beauty. They have been living a life devoid of the promised happiness he made to her yet she never abandoned him.

Cherilus suddenly let out a deep sigh. One of his sons who was playing on the dirt floor put something in his mouth. Cherilus exploded in anger.

"Woman! Take this child off the floor! He's eating the dirt!" he shouted to his wife.

The young woman turned her head toward her husband, unable to understand this sudden exasperation. She left the maize flour porridge she was cooking to lift her one-year-old son from the ground. While at it, she violently gathered the older children, who were still babies, aged three and five. Cherilus took a handkerchief out of his pocket and wiped the runny nose of one of his children. Then he scolded each one of them so loudly that they ran in tears and took refuge in the corner of the house where Solon usually slept.

Smoke, from the indoor cooking, was filling the miserable dwelling, making it hard to see the many pages of magazine and scraps of newspaper plastering the walls. Cherilus was choking with irritation. He needed to calm down. He stepped out of his hovel to breathe some fresh air, but a foul stench from the stagnating dirty water in a nearby gutter reached his nose. He greeted a few neighbors whose bodies were worn out by work and fatigue. The dwellers of this slum were laborers returning home and bringing back their continued struggles, disappointments, but also the latest news of the city. Their bursts of laughter, their unbridled shouts, their arguments, the sounds of crying children, blended together in a dizzying cacophony.

Cherilus lowered his head for a moment to look at the dry skin of his aching feet. How was he going to get out of this neighborhood? He managed a smile, though. After all,

Solon was his tenant. The money he will soon win could be the needed catalyst for escaping his precarious situation.

"If he doesn't tire himself out," he thought quietly, "Solon could pocket his 2,500 *gourdes* ($500 USD). I'll tell him to pay his rent in full for the year. I'll be able to convince him to save money and not to spend it. With that rent, I'll be able to buy a wheelbarrow and rent it out to burden bearers in *Croix-des-Bossales* farmers' market. I'll convince Solon to invest."

Since he started having children, Cherilus could not put away money under the single large mattress filled with rags that he was sharing with his wife and his youngest child. The business capital he needed must therefore come from Solon's rent.

"Of course," Cherilus continued to think, "when I own this wheelbarrow, I'll work to grow the business enough to buy more. And with the money, I'll get a boat that will bring goods back and forth from Port-au-Prince to *Jérémie*."

Cherilus knew that, with his large family, he would not be able to live in two cities. To successfully carry out his future endeavor, he would need help. He taught about his acquaintances in *Jérémie*. Even though he knew many people there, there were very few he could rely on. Many of his family members and his old neighbors envied him for moving to the capital, believing he had already made a fortune in this modern city.

Cherilus crossed his arms over his chest, his eyes distant. He stared at the canal filled with stagnant water until someone's name came to his mind.

"Ah!" he remembered. "Yeah. I have my *monkonpè* (a good friend) who can help me. I've done so much for him. I don't think he would dare to refuse me."

Cherilus was happy with his plan. He stood up, stretched out, and yawned. The pleasant smell of the familiar maize flour porridge, flavored with a hint of vanilla, drew him back inside his hovel for a moment of calm. As soon as he reentered, he took charge of distributing the food to the family. He poured two large ladles into an enameled plate, spreading the liquid in all directions to allow it to cool more quickly. The smile on his face drew his children who ran towards him, eager to satisfy their hunger.

Cherilus went to bed early that night with an almost empty stomach. He could not sleep. His mind was racing, suddenly exploring all the opportunities Solon's 2,500 *gourdes* ($500 USD) were offering. He felt he had to become a genuine support to his friend's participation from now on, to ensure he won the contest.

At dawn, Cherilus got up, but felt a little numb. While his family was still sleeping, he took a cup of water, washed his face, and gargled the rest. Quickly, he put on his clothes and headed to the *Bord-de-Mer,* eager to see what a new tomorrow will bring.

The venue would have been almost empty if it were not for Mr. Gomez, the first responder team, the dancers, two commentators from 4VRW radio station, and a reduced orchestra playing some lively *méringues.* Parents and friends gave up their seats to night owls or early risers who, like Cherilus, were desperate to see who had given up and who was still holding on.

Even if Shilette's eyes was telling otherwise. Solon, for his part, was one of those who was still holding on; those whose hope was the driving force that kept them going. His father's drum, once the rhythm of his childhood, was drowned by the sound of the future singing in his ears. Solon was getting more confident as he studied everything the "experts", like Clifford F. Mayer, were doing. He followed and then meticulously copied their techniques, knowing that each mastered move was one step closer to achieving his dreams.

“What's this guy's partner like?” Solon inquired with Shilette a few hours earlier.

"She doesn't talk much to us. During her morning break, she eats and go to sleep."

"Ah... Okay..." Solon said with a vague expression. "Well, you'll do like her. During our breaks, we'll close our eyes to shut out what's going on around us. Even while eating, keep your eyes closed. Do you understand me?"

Solon was so focused on the instructions he was giving that his short teeth suddenly resembled small sharp blades. The unusual severity on his face caught Shilette off guard, revealing a man whose determination she had never imagined.

Therefore, that morning when Cherilus found them on the dance floor, they were still moving. Shilette kept pace, even though Solon seemed to be managing the movements. Before leaving for work that day, Cherilus watched them for a long time. He was sure of their victory. Their endurance and complicity were evident, transforming them into dancers who had nothing to envy from others.

Yet, Shilette chose not to complain even if she was feeling increasingly tired. She drew inspiration from her mother's strength, who, despite the weight of age and life's setbacks, never complained in her presence. Solon increasingly admired this resilience and the faint smile that tirelessly played on the young girl's lips.

"You never told me how you ended up in Port-au-Prince?" he asked her at this point.

Indeed, since the contest started, Solon was unable to speak to Shilette, even during the short breaks. And yet, intrigued by her silent resilience, Solon wanted to discover the trials that shaped this inexperienced young girl's somewhat calm character.

Caught off guard by this interest, Shilette hesitated.

"Why would I tell you things like that?" she asked, lowering her eyes.

"Because you know everything about me... You know I know how to read and can write poems like all the great poets of *Jérémie*."

Shilette let out a small, mischievous smile.

"*Ti chelbè* (pretentious little fellow)!" she mocked.

"You too can be a *chelbèz*, a girl as beautiful as the morning dew."

Despite the complicity that hours of dancing created between them, Shilette felt embarrassed by the compliment that was delivered smoothly in an overly sweet tone. Bothered by such directness, she moved a little further away from Solon.

"Sorry, sorry...I didn't want to scare you. I just want to know why you left *Cayes-Jacmel*."

The young girl not being accustomed by such direct interrogation responded slowly and cautiously.

"To go to school."

"Really?" Solon asked in surprise. "And why have you never mentioned that?"

"Because I've never been actually to school..."

This revelation threw Solon into a state of confusion that slowed his movements.

"What?"

"We were lied to..." Shilette replied, bitterly.

Solon swallowed, surprised by the expression on the girl's face. She was suddenly saddened by the memory of her trapped youth.

"My mother worked as a janitor for this woman and cleaned her store every day in the city of *Cayes-Jacmel*. That woman had a sister who lived in Port-au-Prince and who said she wanted to help the child of a poor family. My mother believed her and saw an opportunity for me to get a good education. Mother then took me to the capital to that woman..."

Solon was listening to her nightmarish story with such attention that he felt the young girl's pain. His pain grew even more acute when he thought of his own brothers and sisters, perhaps also doomed to such a future if he does not find a way to help them.

"How did you manage to get out from this situation?" he asked.

"My mother came one day to bring some produce to this woman as a way of thanking her for taking good care of me. She had the shock of her life when she saw how skinny and weary I was."

"So, you went back to *Cayes-Jacmel*?"

"For just a while. When the president announced on the radio that he wanted to celebrate the capital's two hundredth anniversary, we moved back here."

Solon looked at the young girl tenderly.

"If you want, I can teach you how to read and write. I can show you everything I know," he gently offered.

"Really?" Shilette asked excitedly.

"Yes."

Shillette's eyes brightened up; her steps became light as if she was floating on clouds.

"Finally! I can make my dream come true!" she exclaimed.

"Your dream?" Solon repeated, confused.

"Yes! My dream of becoming a great international singer like Lumane Casimir!" Shilette blurted out as if it was a given.

Solon gazed at her admiringly, amazed by the young girl's sudden cheerfulness. Like them, Lumane Casimir, now so popular singer, arrived in Port-au-Prince with a dream. She came to the city with only the baggage of a peerless voice and a desire to live life with all it can offer.

"Is that why you're always humming her lyrics?"

Shilette nodded in. Solon moved closer to her. He starred deeply at her. He wanted her to know how serious his offer was.

"You're right. You can't spend the rest of your life cooking for workers. You need to know how to read and write. As soon as this marathon ends, we'll begin the lessons. I'll help you achieve your dream."

CHAPTER 9
Fifty hours…

Shilette was not the only one who had dreams. For Lucien Victorin Cantave, his children's participation in the competition was a moment of renewal. Every hour of their toil was a way to release the pressures, to ease the burden of his financial worries, and to inject a degree of happiness into his grueling daily life.

Invigorated by the anticipated success of his kids, on the morning of the third day, Victorin went to his grocery store with a different spirit. He felt strong. His hope infused him of energy. He no longer lost his breath walking just a few steps. That day, in fact, he walked tirelessly from his house in *Lalue* to *Portail Saint-Joseph*; a walking distance of almost an hour for him.

After inspecting the grocery store, Victorin sat on one of the high straw chairs, watching his wife and Alfred handling the customers. The memory of their humble beginnings and their resilience made him feel proud.

He and his wife worked hard to get this business up and running! Launched in the middle of World War II, *Au*

Petit Dindon represented a risky financial gamble for them. It was a time when flour became a rare commodity, cooking oil reached exorbitant prices, and soap, usually imported from Europe, was impossible to find. Yet the grocery store became a symbol of hope in a country besieged by shortages. It swept away fears, reawakened the patriotism, and quadrupled the desire of all to survive.

With all their savings and a few *'kout ponya'* (overwhelming high interest loans) that seemed to bind them almost for life to their debtors, the Cantave couple rented this small room overlooking a busy street at *Portail Saint-Joseph*. They paid for Marguerite, their eldest daughter, to learn how to make various handcrafted items like homemade soap. Then, they designed the layout and built the shelves in the store; they even invented a functional counter-door. Every Friday, from the vendors that came to sell their products at *Gare du Nord* farmers' market, they bought food stuffs, various grains, resold them or transformed the grains into flour. And so, little by little, *Au Petit Dindon* became one of the most popular grocery stores in the commercial district of *Portail Saint-Joseph*...

The sound of a van being parked in front of the grocery store pulled out Victorin from his nostalgia. He leaned over to see who was coming and saw the baker about to enter to make his daily delivery of bread. Victorin climbed down from the straw chair to meet him.

"Vic," said the baker, surprised. "You're in great shape!"

Victorin let out a nervous smile before sharing with the baker the fear and uncertainty he and his family faced over the past six months; his unstable blood pressure and his accident forced him to take an unintentional rest.

"I'm a miracle from God, Cameo... I almost died, you know."

The baker placed a caring hand on Victorin's shoulder.

"Don't talk like that. You are a model of determination for all of us. Your family, just like the country, needs you!"

Victorin let out a melancholic smile, which quickly faded. He turned to Alfred and made a gesture that meant a lot to him. He signaled to his son to bring a rolled-up envelope. Then, he opened the counter door to allow the baker to enter.

A hint of relief appeared on Victorin's face. Head held high, he handed the envelope to the baker.

"This is the money we owed you, as well as the amount for today's delivery. We're even now."

"Victorin, my friend," Cameo protested, "we've known each other for so long. You shouldn't have rushed like this."

Victorin felt lighter, however. This was a weight off his back; one less debt on his honor. The store owner breathed deeply as he pulled up his trousers. The money he just paid cleared the path for optimism, reopened some doors he had closed on his future plans.

Victorin put a hand on the baker's shoulder and led him out of the store. They walked side by side toward Cameo's van. He recalled the day when everything almost took a turn for the worst. That day started well, though. Free from the constraints of everyday life, they talked about their respective families, about expanding their business, becoming thus more appealing to tourists visiting the capital.

"You remember," Victorin recalled, "we vaguely talked about a pickup truck that would help me with the groceries."

"Ah!" said the baker. "That's true. I know someone who's selling one right now."

"Really? How much is it?

"2,500 *gourdes* ($500 USD). It's a 1939 Ford pickup truck in perfect condition. It has a good engine and new tires. The transmission is excellent, especially on slopes."

Victorin ran feverishly his hand through his hair. 2,500 *gourdes* represented half the amount his children would win. A substantial sum every coin of which would help pay off their debts. More than just numbers, it was also the symbol of four days of sacrifice Emilio and Emilia were making on behalf of the entire family.

"Man!" said Victorin. "It's expensive!"

"Yes, but imagine," Cameo said quietly as he moved closer to his friend. "With this car, you'll no longer need to bother your children to go pick up merchandise here and there. No more workers to bring your goods. You'll be able to go to the warehouse yourself to buy what you need in bulk. Your handling costs will be cut in half."

Even though the offer was tempting, the questions raised by this investment were racing through Victorin's mind.

"But... what about maintenance? Spare parts must be costly."

"They have a garage," the baker started reassuringly, "a garage that specializes in Ford trucks. In fact, one of the mechanics is my cousin. I'll tell him to always give you a reduced price."

Victorin bowed his head, longing for those years when he was in perfect health; when his wife, younger than him, had more energy to follow him in his intrepid dreams. Victorin rubbed the back of his neck. He was torn between fear and hope. He felt as if every time a window opened onto a promising future, he encountered a new challenge that forced him to draw on a reserve of courage whose depth he was unaware of. Victorin reflected briefly, breathing slowly to chase away his doubts. Nothing ventured, nothing gained. Such was life…

"Where can we see this truck?" he finally asked.

"On *Des Miracles* Street, across from the National Bank. Tomorrow afternoon, around 4 p.m., I can take you there."

"All right," Victorin replied. "Come pick me up at my house."

The baker was about to leave when *Madan* Vic, who had no idea what her husband's conversation was about, gestured from inside the store.

"Cameo, if you're not in a hurry, eat with us," she said. "We are having *royals* for lunch. Or at least have a cup of coffee."

"No thank you for the coffee. I've already had two cups today. But I never turn down a *royal*. I'll have one before I leave."

With an expert hand, *Madan* Vic took pieces of flat rounded crispy cassava, drizzled them with spicy cabbage sauce to soften them before spreading on top peanut butter and some pre-cooked herring. With a slight smile on her lips, she put some watercress on the cassava and folded each into a sandwich. She gave a *royal* to the baker, who thanked her before continuing his rounds.

Cameo's had barely left when Liliane cheerfully arrived for her mid-day break. The sailor collar of her navy-blue striped blouse stood out against the immaculate white of the rest of her school uniform. Even after a morning at school, it looked as if it just has been ironed.

The young girl clung to her father's neck and planted a resounding kiss on his cheek that lit up his face.

"*Royals*!" she cried, licking her lips in delight.

Anticipating one of the delicious herring smelling sandwiches, Victorin salivated expectedly. However, he watched his wife making a simpler version excluding many of the previous ingredients. Carefully, *Madan* Vic took two slices of cassava like before, moistened them with the cabbage sauce, and then topped them with a few watercress leaves. She arranged them on a beautiful enamel plate and served them to her husband.

"But," Victorin protested, "this is definitely not a Royal Air Force! Without herring, without *manba* (peanut butter), without peppers?!"

Madan Vic stared at her husband with a certain discouragement. Though, she knew how fond her husband was of herring, cod, and other salted foods, nevertheless she insisted on following the doctor's orders. Victorin needed to stay away from anything that could affect his high blood pressure.

"Remember," she said in a tone that was both gentle and authoritative, "the doctor said you should cut back on salt until you're completely recovered."

With a serious look on his face, Victorin fell silent. He, however, noticed Alfred and Liliane who were smiling mischievously at the interaction with their mother. If there was one thing Victorin was certain about is, in their twenty-five years of marriage, that he must at all costs avoid getting in his wife's way over minor matters. Even when upset, he knew when to let it go and not to start or prolong an argument.

"Here's the medication for your blood pressure, Dad," Alfred said with a cup of water in hand.

Victorin thanked his son and then tossed a pill down his throat. After all, he wanted to do everything he could to stabilize his health. His head was filled with so many projects.

Victorin pulled himself back onto one of the high chairs, chewing slowly after taking a bite of cassava sandwich, his gaze fixed on the street. He was now thinking about the twins, from whom he had not heard for hours.

"So, what about the competition today?" he asked his son, glancing anxiously at an old clock he just installed in the grocery store not long ago.

"Oh no! It's past noon!" exclaimed Alfred, realizing they missed the updates.

Liliane could not believe she forgot about the competition. She took a bite, at her *royal,* wiped her fingers, and turned the radio dial on 4VRW station frequencies. The news anchor was just presenting the sponsors' advertisements.

"This segment of the marathon was brought to you by Good Year Tires! Upgrade your ride with the new Super Cushion tires! Good Year's Super Cushion, for a safer car, for a smoother ride."

Madan Vic let out a sigh, anxiety deepening the color of her eyes. Not knowing what her children were going through at the *Bord-de-Mer* was raising her level of impatience.

Alfred felt a little guilty for having failed in his self-imposed mission of keeping the whole family informed on what was happening at the marathon. He took a single bite of the rest of his *roya*l and started to walk away.

"I'm going to see if the merchant of fabrics on the corner of the street received today's newspaper."

"Go quickly before apprehension makes your mother loses her composure and consciousness," Victorin teased, trying to lighten the atmosphere filled with worry.

Alfred soon returned with the newspaper in his hand.

"This morning at a quarter to 10, the President toured the construction sites of the International Exhibition and honored the dancers of the 100-Hour Grand National Dance Marathon with his visit. The remaining 21 dancing couples gave the President an indescribable amount of applause."

Madan Vic, who was all ears, scratched her face with a puzzled expression.

"Well, what if the competition ends with more than one winner? Have they thought of that?"

Alfred recalled a part in the rules he read the night of the contest's launched.

"If no dancer manages to beat the 100-hour record," he patiently explained to his mother, "the 5,000 *gourdes* will be divided among the three finalists who come closest to 100 hours."

"But," Liliane added, "for these three finalists to be considered, they must exceed 80 hours."

"And, if two or more dancers reach 100 hours?"

"The competition continues until we have a winner," Alfred said.

Victorin crossed his arms over his chest. The competition was halfway through the 100 hours. He pondered the possibility of his children being the winners among the twenty-one couples who remained. With a defiant look in his eyes and a slight smile on his lips, Victorin thought about how much of those 5,000 *gourdes* he could set aside for advertisements. The commercials on the radio since the start of the contest stirred up his ideas.

Even though he was unable to install a neon sign yet, at least he could harness the growing power of advertising. He was aware that the majority of his customers were illiterate. He knew, as such, that they would be more motivated by what they heard than what is written in French. When he would buy the pickup truck, he would install a radio on top of it that would broadcast the advertisements in Creole through a loudspeaker. Not to mention that he could have the name of his grocery store written on the body of this car.

Victorin enjoyed the last bite of his *royal;* his simple meal suddenly tasted a lot better. Life is sweeter when projects are more attainable. Pushed by a surge of optimism, Victorin quickly grabbed a sheet of paper and began to write down his slogan:

"Oye! Oye! *Au Petit Dindon*!
Au Petit Dindon grocery store at *Portail Saint-Joseph*!
A store that always sells FRESH produce!
Where the stock is continually replenished
and the customer is ALWAYS satisfied!"

Out of curiosity, Alfred came closer seeing his father's unbridled happiness. His excitement and plans lit a fire among the rest of the family.

"Oh," said Alfred, "it would be nice to add: 'Before you go anywhere else, come to *Au Petit Dindon* Grocery Store where a warm welcome awaits you!'"

"We must also remember to list all the things we sell," suggested *Madan* Vic.

Victorin smiled. In a very short time, Emilio and Emilia would win. How he would have loved to support them with his presence! But with a heavy heart, he quickly realized that his physical condition would not withstand the walk from *Portail Saint-Joseph* to *Les Palmistes* and then the same distance back home.

"Shouldn't Marguerite be here already?" he asked.

"Not necessarily," his wife replied. "Sometimes she comes after bringing the food."

Marguerite had indeed fallen behind in her duties that day. Assigned to the crucial task of feeding Emilio and Emilia during the marathon, she had to rush straight to the club.

When she arrived around 1:30 PM, amidst a crowd of supporters, Emilio and Emilia were in the final minutes, which would mark six hours of straight dancing for them.

As he was about to take his break, Emilio noticed Solon's fatigue. The young man physical condition was starting to attract his attention, as he noticed him earlier eating only a clear beef foot broth with no starch in it.

"Is it time for you to stop?" Emilio asked him, still moving.

"No, not yet. But soon we'll have rounded three hours," Solon said breathlessly.

"Then take fifteen minutes and come join us in front of the women's quarters. We'll save you a bite to eat."

"Thank you," said Solon, swallowing.

When Marguerite saw her siblings coming her way, she unpacked the food. The smell of the purée of red beans and white rice made the exhausted Emilia close her eyes in an adulterated joy. The spinach, carrot pieces, and a few *donmbwèy* (savory dumplings) floating in the purée of red beans were like the compensation she and Emilio needed.

"A friend and his partner are going to eat with us," Emilio simply announced.

Marguerite raised her eyebrows, fascinated by her brother's ability to make friends even during a marathon. The young woman looked at the food and was glad she thought of securing it tightly.

"No problem," she said. "As long as they don't have big appetites, we can share with them."

Emilio poured the purée of red beans over his rice. The number 18 gleaming on his back, he hunched over with fatigue; he buried his head in his bowl, feasting.

Slumped beside him, Emilia took off her shoes and rubbed her feet with a frown. She really needed these thirty minutes of rest, her tiredness growing ever greater.

"Your feet are swelling," Marguerite commented.

"Yes. I'm also starting to get a bit of cramping and a slight migraine."

"I felt that headache too," Emilio admitted. "Maybe we were too hungry."

Even from some distance, Emilia's fatigue did not escape Dr. Wallon's vigilant gaze. From his table, the doctor was closely monitoring all the dancers, including those who were resting. He stood up and walked over to perform a thorough examination of the twins.

"Let me see your feet," the doctor said to Emilia.

Dr. Wallon's unexpected appearance in the group startled everyone. Emilia looked up at him with an apologetic way as she listened to his diagnosis.

"These are signs of acidosis," the doctor concluded. "That mean that there is an acid-base imbalance. It's your body that is beginning to react to fatigue. We'll treat this quickly."

The doctor checked first Emilia's blood pressure, then her brother's. Then he checked their breathing and pulse. At the doctor's signal, one of the nurses arrived, elevated the girl's feet, and massaged them with precise movements.

Emilia instinctively closed her eyes, letting a sense of well-being take over her feet and tired limbs. Her reaction brought a broad smile to the doctor's face.

"You'll feel even better in a short time," he said.

Dr. Wallon's kind face comforted the twins and eased Marguerite's fears, who, for a distressing moment, thought this was the beginning of the end for the twins' participation in the marathon.

Yet, as soon as the doctor left, Emilio became preoccupied again. Their dedication on the dance floor worn their shoes, making the soles barely recognizable. Nevertheless, they must last until the end. Their family's honor depended on their victory. Emilio would not accept the humiliation his parents would suffer at the hands of their creditors. He was determined to win the 5,000 *gourdes* to regain their peace.

The worried look on her brother's face did not escape Marguerite.

"My shoes are more comfortable than yours," she said to her sister. "I'll give them to you."

"That would be nice, but they have heels. When Alfred comes later, could you ask Mom to send me the ones she usually wears to the farmers' market? They must be in better condition now than mine."

As the siblings continued to chat, Adrienne Dolan passed by, attracting the group's attention. Her look was showing authority and ambition. The number 27 on her back, she was holding a bowl containing her meal. She adjusted her large dark glasses before exchanging a wave with the group. Intimidated by her appearance, Emilia simply waved back.

"Who is she?" Marguerite whispered.

"A widow," Emilia replied in a tone of respect and admiration. "Her husband recently died, leaving her with a young child."

"How sad!"

Marguerite leaned over to look at the competitor who was sitting down into the women's section on her camp bed.

"But why is she the one wearing the number?" she asked puzzled.

"She's the one in charge."

Marguerite did not understand how a woman with a dance partner could so openly take control. Was that this despotic attitude that perhaps killed her husband? She wondered. While it was true that since the end of the war, women increasingly asserted themselves into societal affairs, Marguerite remained convinced that certain tasks belonged only to men, while women should simply assist them.

"And she thinks she can win the grand prize?" Marguerite asked ironically.

"I think she can," Emilia replied thoughtfully.

Ever since she saw her at the first meeting held at the club, Emilia never stopped spying on Adrienne Dolan. Like her brother and herself, number 27 knew the relaxation techniques that soothed fatigue. She controlled her movements and seemed to maintain her concentration intact despite the other competitors and the crowd's countless reactions.

Emilio was paying no attention to his sisters' conversation. He was still gobbling his purée of red beans when Solon and Shilette arrived. He gestured for them to come forward. Timidly, Solon took two chairs and placed them near the group.

"Come on, my friend! Eat with us!" Emilio encouraged.

Touched by her brother's invitation, Marguerite regretted not having brought more food.

"It's very little," she said.

"It's a lot for us," Solon thanked. "It'll help us to continue until the next break."

With a slight smile on her lips, Marguerite poured spoonful of food into each dish. Emilia, after finishing up, passed her spoon to Shilette. Touched by such kindness, Shilette warmly thanked her new friends. Solon was also moved, his eyes shining with gratitude.

"Thank you, Emilio. It's God who told you to invite us."

"Why?" Emilia asked, intrigued.

"Our last break was over three hours ago. We only had a little broth that my friend brought us. It was not enough for one person, but we had to share it between us. And it was all we had eaten since dawn."

"My mother was supposed to bring us food," Shilette said in a faint voice. "She's usually never late, but now we've been waiting for her for over an hour, and it's starting to worry me."

"She must have customers," Solon tried to soothe.

"What does your mother do?" Marguerite asked.

"She sells food at the various construction sites in and around the waterfront area."

"Really?" said Emilia who was surprised and happy to have something in common with the young girl. "We're in business too. Our parents have a grocery store at *Portail Saint-Joseph*. It's called *Au Petit Dindon*."

Shillette's face lit up with astonishment.

"Oh!" she said enthusiastically. "When we have money, that's where my mother buys the soap she really likes."

Emilio got up from his chair to adjust his clothes, giving his sister a knowing smile.

"Well, Miss Marguerite Cantave, here, is the creator of the soaps your mother loves so much."

Shillette's eyes opened up wide.

"It's nothing. I already have a new recipe that will include a special oil for dry skin..." said Marguerite, taking the opportunity to share her future projects.

Solon watched Marguerite speaking, a smile playing at the corners of his lips. A wonderful idea just struck his imagination. Rosa has not yet opened her own business, while the Cantaves owned a well-known store for years. If he wanted to introduce his parents' coffee to Port-au-Prince, it was with them that he had to start the business. He has been thinking about a way for a few days and finally found it.

"Do you also sell coffee?" he asked.

"No," replied Emilio.

Solon's heart leaped in his chest.

"My parents are coffee growers in *Jérémie,*" he blurted out without hesitation. "We have a small plot where we plant high-quality beans. Our dream, God willing, is to be able to export them abroad."

Surprised by this unexpected detail, Emilio listened attentively to Solon. He suddenly realized how often his parents served coffee to friends or neighborhood merchants without offering it to their customers. If they sold it, they could make a good profit, especially since they would not have any competitors located nearby.

"The reputation of the coffee coming out of *Grande-Anse* region is well known. The one your parents grow must be excellent."

Marguerite nodded.

"Do you sell it in the city?" she asked.

"No, not yet. But if you like, we could start in your grocery store," Solon offered courageously.

"You have to let us taste it first," Emilia said.

"No problem," Solon replied enthusiastically.

This business project plunged Solon into some serious mental calculation. If his parents' business can not realize their export dream, it was because they could not reach directly the big merchants themselves. The resellers were pocketing the largest profit from their harvests. But if he could manage the deliveries himself, his parents could do away with these middlemen.

"I'll bring you a sample," he continued, pleased by the glimmer of hope.

"It's one of my mother's favorite drinks," Emilia revealed.

"So, she'll love the fruity scent and the very sweet taste of our coffee!"

As they spoke, Solon, Shilette, and Emilia also stood up while Marguerite was pilling the dishes on top of each other. The fifty hours they just announced brought them back to the reality of the marathon. Solon and his partner thanked the Cantave children again for their generosity. The few spoonsful of food they ate were like rain falling on a parched land.

As Shilette and Emilia walked toward the dance floor, discussing soaps and embroidery. Solon moved closer to Emilio. The shared meal and this coffee business project established a bond between the two men that made Solon want to know more about his new friends.

"This is the first time I'm participating in a competition like this," he confessed.

"Us too," replied Emilio. "But I have the feeling there are some among us who are not at their first attempt."

"Like number 60," Solon disclosed quietly. "They call him Clifford F. Mayer. They say he is a regular at these competitions and that his last participation was in 1945."

"That's unfair!" Emilio retorqued with irritation. "They should never have allowed inexperienced people like us to compete against them."

"I can't stop thinking the same thing," said Solon.

As they walked toward the dance floor, Clifford F. Mayer was still driving the audience crazy. They were applauding him relentlessly. Several businesses were associating their brands with his name. The chief commentator of radio 4VRW could not refrain from comparing Mayer's resilience to Pontiac cars.

"Like the beautiful Pontiac," he shouted into the microphone, "no one can beat Mayer! Yes, dear listeners, as they say in the United States: Dollar for Dollar, You Just Can't Beat a Pontiac! If you believe in strength, durability, and beauty, don't hesitate to go choose your favorite model! Let it be known that Clifford F. Mayer, number 60, is your favorite competitor in the 100-Hour Dance competition then you'll receive a discount on the Pontiac of your choice!"

Dancing not far from the news anchor, Max Belmont was smiling, fascinated by the audience shouting its admiration for his friend. For his part, he felt he would not make it to the next hour. Yet, while Belmont and his partner were reaching the end of the adventure, they did not want in any way leave looking weak. Like Christian, his presence was the result of long discussions with his parents. Anxious to keep their reputation and that of the family business intact, Belmont knew that his departure had to be done with dignity.

Max Belmont and his partner stopped, nodded their heads, revealed a winning smile on their lips. The young man made himself tall as he firmly took his partner's hand. He walked over to Clifford F. Mayer, who was still dancing, and gave him a hug.

"What's going on?" Mayer asked, confused.

"We're leaving," Belmont replied simply with a small smile. "All the best, my friend!"

Max Belmont walked over and handed Mr. Carrey his number 55 under the gaze of the crowd. While the young man's withdrawal seemed inconsequential, for Emilio and Solon it was a tactical victory. For them, it was one less couple which absence would allow them to better match number 60's every move.

Emilio kept an eye on Mayer. Since Solon's revelations, he has been looking for a strategy to defeat him. He noticed his few gray hairs, the lines appearing on his forehead, his slight double chin...

"Don't worry," he reassured quietly, moving closer to Solon. "He may have more stamina than number 55, but he's not unbeatable. I'm sure there's something we can work with."

"Like what?" Solon asked, sounding interested.

"We're younger than him. He can't have the same strength he had in 1945."

"Right…"

Shilette and Emilia were following the conversation between the two young men without understanding. However, even if they did not dare question them, the seriousness on their faces made them frown and pay closer attention.

"I noticed he closes his eyes as soon as he takes a break," Solon continued.

"So that's it!" Emilio replied. "He's recharging his batteries. There are also the massages and vitamins he's taking."

"But why does he have to swallow all those pills like a chicken eating seed?" Solon asked.

The question made Shilette and Emilia giggle.

"Remember the explanations we were given during the pre-contest meetings," Emilio said. "Those massages and vitamins are important to invigorate our bodies and chase away fatigue. I think we should start taking them too."

"Especially the massages," Emilia added, remembering the sense of well-being she felt under the nurse's expert hands.

"Exactly," her brother said. "We'll also continue at the same pace, without doing too much effort. Okay?"

Solon readily agreed to follow Emilio's advice. All though feeling a growing heaviness in his legs and lower back, he was not going to give up.

CHAPTER 10
Sixty hours...

Other eliminations followed number 55's. This caused mixed feelings among the remaining competitors which drained their energy and vitality. However, if for some, like Emilio, it was a proof that they were getting closer to victory; yet, for many others, the pressure made their movements heavier and the fatigue pressing.

A unanimous "Oh!" from the audience shook the room loudly with every abandoning pairs. Two other couples, whom the crowd has been following closely, dropped out. Another, whose partner was faltering, went to Dr. Wallon's who informed them they were no longer fit to continue.

Despite their understanding Emilio and Solon were gripped by the collective surprise. Aside from Mayer, the two other eliminated couples were among those who showed a competitive spirit. They were among those who knew how to keep up their stamina without taking a break.

Yet, despite their technique, they have not been able to stay in the battle.

These successive withdrawals fueled Solon's determination. Each elimination added, though, to the heaviness on his own body. The heaviness was felt on his shoulders, his hips, and his calves. The heaviness was right now being materializing as a sudden pain that shot straight up from the soles of his feet to his buttocks. Solon held his breath, biting his lower lip as he raised his head, his eyes wide open. His forehead beaded with sweat. He tried to keep his discomfort under control. There was no way he was going to give up. Shilette needed him as much as he needed her.

Yet, despite Solon's stoicism, the young girl's gaze was blank, her eyes scanning the other dancers and the crowd. She was like a flickering candle about to go out. She was barely speaking, even becoming visibly breathless. Her feet were dragging; hunger and thirst were making each of her movements clumsier. She was letting herself be guided by Solon like a child without willpower until she saw Rosa making her way through the audience.

"Here's my mom!" she announced with a slight surge of energy.

Solon looked up and indeed saw Rosa, her stern face contrasting with the cheerfulness of the crowd.

It's been some hours that the lady merchant was trying to identify one of the participants whose name was on everyone's lips. But that evening, she was determined to find who that Mayer was. When she got closer to the dance floor, she focused her attention on the young man. Every detail she noted was confirming his mastery of dance techniques and his ability to win it all. Yet Rosa did not agree to let her daughter participate in a dance marathon simply for nothing; just to count the experience as a credit to her achievements. Those hundred hours deprived Rosa of Shilette's invaluable help in her business. She must finish the task of winning her 2,500 *gourdes* ($500 USD).

Rosa has been looking for a way to get a break from her grueling life. She was no longer very young, and her body was tired from hoping from construction sites to construction sites. Her cooking was celebrated now; and she knew that wherever she settled down her business, she would succeed. She was even more certain of this because she closely examined the tastes of many tourists who arrived in the country in search of new experiences. If she transformed the front porch of her small house in *Carrefour* into a restaurant, she knew the business would definitely flourish. For the exhausting life Rosa led, those 2,500 *gourdes* ($500 USD) were more than a prize. That money was a gleaming view of the future. It was the saving rain that needed to fall on Rosa's desperate arid life.

The lady merchant curled her lips and let out a "hmm," sign of the determination and frustration rising within her. Slowly, she turned her attention to Solon and her daughter, searching for flaws in their movements that Mayer could take advantage of.

Solon had a faint smile on his lips as he looked at Rosa's stern expression, seeing behind that mask all the tenderness the merchant felt for her daughter. Shilette's story made it clear to him. Rosa's rough manner was ultimately just a way for her to protect her daughter.

"How are you two doing?" Rosa asked as Solon approached her.

"I'm tired!" complained Shilette.

"I brought you both some food. Stop dancing now," Rosa ordered.

Solon looked at the clock to check the time before informing the judge that he was taking another ten-minute break. Before entering the women's quarters with her daughter, Rosa took out of a bag containing a banana and three loaves of bread. She cut open the loaves one by one.

She spread peanut butter inside of both, then handed them to Solon. The *manba* (peanut butter) was greasy and jelly-like. Solon thanked her and went to a corner of the men's quarters.

A few other competitors were resting. Some stretched out on their camp beds, others sitting on chairs against the wall. Solon found a chair and threw himself on it, his legs as heavy as lead. His toes needed to be freed from the constraints of the shoes, but the fear of the smell of sweat they would discharge dissuaded him.

Solon held two breads in one hand and devoured the third, each bite swallowed with eyes closed. He was temporarily disconnected from the anxious reality of the moment and his body and spirit were being uplifted. The bread in his mouth transformed into a *konparèt* (sweet biscuit made from sugarcane syrup), he loved since childhood.

He thought about the time and the many hours that have already passed. From the dance floor, he has seen many sunrises and sunsets. Solon was exhausted, but he was in the race of his life. Tired or not, he could not give up.

Memories of long ago flooded his mind. At a young age, he was forced to dropout from school. Fortunately, he had time to study geometry, symmetry, and spatial reasoning, skills he was now appling every day as a gardener. It was also during these school years that he discovered poetry, beautiful verses he learned by heart. On Sunday afternoons, it was on *Place Dumas* in *Jérémie* that one could find him. He was always on the lookout for a poet who was proposing a piece. He studied their pronunciations, their deliveries, the tone of the rhymes, and the cluster of the expressed ideas. He was learning how to establish emotional connections through words…

Solon straightened up and felt renewed; his eyes were still closed and a smile on his lips. His part of the 5,000 *gourdes* was going to change his future and that of his family. His parents' hard work and professional ethics would be acknowledged. His younger brothers and sisters would follow a different path, that of success.

When Solon finally opened his eyes, he felt the piercing gaze of a person. Indeed, sitting next to him, a competitor has been staring at him, probably for a long time; but he too seemed immersed in deep thought.

This man was Christian whom since the beginning of the competition noticed Solon. The young man's dignified bearing and resilience intrigued him conspicuously. For a moment, he thought of the walkathon his parents told him about; he thought of those years when the stock market crashed in the States, when the quest for survival brought out the violent desperation of people in the pursuit of life necessities.

Christian slowly tore his eyes away from Solon to take a sip of his *Cola Couronne*. Despite himself, he felt an unexpected connection. A deep curiosity took hold of him and forced him to find a way to start the conversation.

"I am exhausted!" he blurted.

Solon did not respond. They were surrounded by other competitors. He did not expect this man, with unruly hair, who was so elegantly drinking a bottle of soda, spoke to him.

Christian returned his insistent gaze on Solon, determined to break the ice.

"I didn't think it would be this tiring... And you?"

Solon finally turned toward Christian, a little of the greasy *manba* (peanut butter) still trickling down the corners of his lips.

"Me neither," he finally replied in a low tone.

Satisfied with this initial sparkle of trust, Christian placed his bottle of soda on the floor. Legs apart, he leaned against his knees, hands clasped, staring straight ahead.

"I just wanted to do it for fun," he confessed.

Solon, with enlarged eyes, was stunned, unable to comprehend what he just heard.

Christian leaned his back against the wall, and crossed his arms over his chest, completely oblivious to the surprise that was evident on Solon's face.

"Yeah... And you? Why are you here?" he asked with a half-smile.

"I have plans..." Solon replied, his expression once again cautious.

Surprised by the answer, Christian stared again at Solon, who was finishing his last piece of bread. What could be the plan of this young man with rough hands? He thought. What more could he want in life than to eat and drink? His appetite was proofs that he was only participating to feed himself. That must be all he planned.

For a moment, Christian remained silent. Around them, those taking their break had distant looks. Those lying on the camp beds seemed to be in pain. Those sitting were becoming shadows of themselves. The initial enthusiasm cooled down. They barely spoke. Glances exchanged now were fierce or shifty. Every breath saved. Smiles becoming rare.

Without knowing why, Christian felt a growing unease within him. From where he was, he could see

Augustin on the dance floor. The latter still dancing, giving the impression of a dislocated puppet. He could no longer identify his movements, wondering if he was performing a *méringue*, an *ibo*, or a *kongo* dance.

"We have plans too," Christian added, as if speaking to himself.

Solon was listening, increasingly confused by the young man's words.

"We're doing this for tuberculosis patients we have never met," Christian continued thoughtfully.

This statement got Solon's full attention. It was not the first time he heard about this disease. Since he moved to *La Saline,* every week someone was becoming the topic of suspicious gossip because of a persistent cough that made their lungs bleed. They were scolded, rejected, abandoned, and even turned away by medical clinics. Solon learned to stay away from them, afraid that their illness could spread to him too... And now, it was for these people that this gentleman was dancing? How could someone go to so much trouble for strangers?

Christian responded with a smirk, as if he heard all of Solon's questions.

At this very moment, an announcement made them both realized that their few minutes breaks were up. The two young men rose from their chairs almost simultaneously. They were of the same height. For a moment, they looked at each other. Christian admired Solon's proud bearing and strong chin. A bright sparkle in the young man's eyes struck him. There was an unspoken and silent understanding.

CHAPTER 11

Seventy Hours...

Since the beginning of the contest, Béatrice's mysterious behavior had been the talk of the town. The youngest of the three travel-and-leisure journalist accompanying Mr. Montrose was not the only one who noticed her regal appearance. In the midst of the crowd, a local reporter discreetly also captured her image.

Among the various photos taken by the reporters was one that surprised Mrs. Grégoire during her daily tea break. After reading the columns depicting the numerous receptions honoring various foreign delegations who came to celebrate Port-au-Prince's two hundredth years, she noted a picture.

"Who's that?" she asked.

"She looks like Adeline de Roseraie," replied Marie-Cécile, who was munching on a chocolate madeleine.

"I doubt it's her," her sister corrected confidently. "Wasn't she supposed to join her husband in Morocco for his new job assignment?"

Mrs. Grégoire put her cup of lemongrass tea on a small table and brought the newspaper closer to her face.

"You're right. It's not her. This young woman has much clearer eyes and lighter complexion. But she looks strangely like her."

"It's a shame they didn't identify the person," Marie-Cécile commented.

While following the conversation, Mr. Grégoire poured himself a second cup of tea, adding a few sugar cubes to it.

"Thank God it's a different story for us," he said, a proud smile on his lips. "Do you know that the journalists from Florida, who were with Montrose, have already written several articles? They highlighted the involvement of Christian and Augustin."

"Really?" Mrs. Grégoire asked in surprise.

"They mentioned the surnames of the participants, stressing the competition's diversity."

"How can we get a copy?" Marie-Cécile asked enthusiastically.

"Montrose promised to bring us a magazine as soon as he receives it."

"Well, that's fantastic!" exclaimed Mrs. Grégoire happily. "Now for sure, the whole world will see how united our people are! I'm glad that we agreed on letting our children participate! Can you imagine the good that these 5,000 *gourdes* will do for the needy?"

Marie-Agnès was silent, sipping her tea, occasionally biting into a madeleine while reflecting on the columns her father was referring to. The marathon's endless recounting of stories was fueling a renewed interest in Augustin's participation, making her secretly hoping he would win. She volunteered so many times at the Port-au-Prince Sanatorium. She saw the death of so many fathers and mothers, leaving behind a host of orphaned children fending for themselves. How many times has she wanted to play for them a song that would ease their despair! But the fear of being infected kept her from getting too close…

Marie-Agnès sighed. Among all the concerts she gave in the city or abroad for so many years, she regretted of never having the courage, even the thought, to organize a concert for the benefit of the unfortunate tuberculosis patients.

The young lady's features suddenly relaxed. Her memories transported her to her last concert. She remembered the bouquet Augustin sent her. It was the first time he scribbled a message: "To the most beautiful and talented of all pianists..."

Marie-Agnès slowly raised her cup of tea to her lips. Augustin suddenly appeared before her. His well-shaped mustache; the comforting words he always has for all; his well-tailored jackets emphasizing his masculine figure and his attention to detail; the determination he displayed encapsulated all his charms... What a handsome man! Marie-Agnès realized.

The young lady blinked rapidly, trying to shake the picture from her mind. Why has she been having these stupid thoughts over the past few days?! After all, she trivialized, there was nothing extraordinary about this donation to the Sanatorium. It was a donation like any other that anyone could have made if they had the funds.

Marie-Agnès straight up on the *dodine* (rocking-chair) and Marie-Cécile's voice became clearer to her ears.

“I don't know how Christian and Augustin manage to dance for four days and four nights without really resting in a nice, soft bed,” her sister was inquiring.

“They're young. I sincerely hope they'll hold on,” her father replied, with a hint of concern.

Mrs. Grégoire also was hoping her son and Augustin would hold on. Every day her husband sent one of his employees to check on them; they and the Montrose family were making sure that their housekeepers were supplying the dancers and their partners with food and things they needed. Moreover, she and her husband knew Dr. Wallon personally. They knew he was a caring, meticulous doctor who devoted his life in serving the most vulnerable.

"Yesterday," Marie-Cécile began to read the newspaper, "the crowd exceeded the record number of 7,000! Listen to this: 'Elegant ladies, high-ranking officials, Ministers, Senators, Deputies, and foreign visitors came to see this show with their own eyes!'"

Marie-Agnès turned her head slightly toward Mr. Grégoire.

"You were the only one missing, Papa," she emphasized admiringly.

Mrs. Grégoire also shared her eldest daughter's thoughts. So many important people were visiting this marathon. It was perhaps time for her husband and herself to appear. And besides, among the attending high-society ladies, who knows if she might meet the one who would suit her son's bon vivant nature.

Roger Grégoire took the newspaper from Marie-Cécile.

"But where did all these people stand?" he remarked. "The venue must have been literally overflowing."

"When I went with the Volmars, I felt like there were just as many people, if not more."

At this last sentence, Mrs. Grégoire's perked up. A fantastic idea just crossed her mind like a flash of lightning. Gisèle Volmar... Yes, indeed, she did not have to look everywhere for a good match for Christian. Single, free, with a solid education, with European parentage on both sides of her family, and far from being poor, the young lady matched all the criteria.

"Gisèle has grown into a very beautiful young woman," began Mrs. Grégoire with a slightly mischievous air. "Has she finished her nursing classes?"

"No," informed Marie-Cécile. "She's changed her mind. She wants to become a doctor."

"Really?" her mother asked in surprise. "For the better... A very avant-garde young woman!"

"There's nothing avant-garde about it, Mom," declared Marie-Agnès. "Since Dr. Yvonne Sylvain became an obstetrician ten years ago, many women are now entering this field."

"Ah," said Elsa Grégoire. "So, I'm behind the times... And what does Violette want to do?"

"She wants to become an architect," informed Marie-Cécile.

"They're not afraid of anything, those girls," said Mr. Grégoire.

"I admire them," Marie-Cécile replied, shrugging her head. "One must be independent and not rely on a husband for everything."

Surprised by this statement, Mrs. Grégoire stared at her daughter. It was the first time she heard such firm words coming out of her mouth with self-confidence. Despite herself, Elsa Grégoire let out a laugh.

"What do you know, my daughter? Having a husband who loves and cares for you is a privilege beyond measure. For me, marriage has meant independence, my child. You lead a peaceful life surrounded by your children. You are queen in your own home, and you are the one who supports your husband in major decisions. You'll see when I find the right person for you."

Marie-Cécile looked at her mother, horrified by this direct talk of marriage that she never discussed with her parents before. While the idea occasionally crossed her mind, it hardly had the same meaning as the one her mother was expressing. Getting married was supposed to be an adventure for two, an investigation of the world preferably without children at your feet like balls and chains.

In any case, at eighteen, finding the "right person" was far from what Marie-Cécile desired. Ever since Mrs. Volmar and her daughters planted the image of the ideal female of the Haitian intelligentsia in her mind, she spent hours thinking about it. She only received her *brevet* (middle school diploma), while, increasingly, young ladies were reaching the secondary level and even pursuing college studies, like the Volmar girls.

And then, it has been a while since Marie-Cécile has been paying attention to the "peaceful" life her mother led, which her older sister was replicating. It was not what she dreamed for herself. She was more concerned about leaving a legacy for future generations.

"But, Mom, getting married isn't what I want right now," she retorted.

"And what do you want, my daughter?" Mrs. Grégoire asked calmly.

"I'd like to see the world, explore the great possibilities open to women. I don't want a husband to take care of me when I can take care of myself."

Amused, Marie-Agnès was watching her father pretending to read the newspaper, his eyes skimming over the sentences, doing everything he could to avoid joining the discussion.

"And how?" asked Mrs. Grégoire, her tone both tender and admiring of Marie-Cécile's candor. "By working? Why would you embark on such a degradation?"

"But it's absolutely not degradation, Mom! Look at Mrs. Volmar. She works and is still respected. What's wrong with that?"

"Ah!" said her mother, as if she had just caught her in the act. "I knew Lynn was behind this reasoning."

Marie-Agnès exchanged a knowing look with her little sister.

"What would you like to do with your life, darling?" Marie-Agnès asked.

"Dad is in finance and Christian's in accounting... So, I don't see why I can't study business."

Mr. Grégoire wiggled in his chair, suddenly looking more present. Confused, he closed the newspaper to stare at Marie-Cécile. The discovery of her aspirations was a real surprise. If he rarely discussed future plans with his daughters, it was because he was convinced that his wife took care of it. Just like her older sister, Marie-Cécile never shown the slightest feeling of dissatisfaction. She always seemed to want to live life to the fullest. That is why he thought that a simple position in the Guest House he was about to open would suit her if one day she would express the desire to work.

Feeling a deep regret, Roger Grégoire, with a raised eyebrow, watched his daughter as she continued to share her wishes. Even if he understood what Marie-Cécile wanted, he did not see how he could explain to his young adult daughter that she would have to go back and finish her basic education before considering college studies.

Mrs. Grégoire glanced irritably at her husband, who seemed perplexed. She mistook his calm as indifference. She smoothed down her skirt and took a deep breath. Fortunately, Lynn Volmar was not the one ruling her home. She was. Therefore, Marie-Cécile and Marie-Agnès would only take the direction she envisioned for them.

Elsa Grégoire breathed slowly to calm herself down. For the moment, her intention was not to fight the small rebellion she felt brewing in Marie-Cécile. Another case, in which Gisèle was the main character, had just opened; and she was determined to explore it as soon as the competition was over.

"When will this dance competition end?" she asked, trying to trivialize her daughter's desire for higher education.

"In less than two days," announced Marie-Agnès.

Mrs. Gregoire's question was like the excuse her husband was waiting for to put an end to the discussion between her and his daughter.

"I'll check for myself this afternoon how Christian and Augustin are doing," he hastened to say. "More than ever, they need our support."

However, when the afternoon arrived, Roger Grégoire had no time for anything that was not already pinned in his agenda. After an intense day at the Central Bank, he had a frugal dinner at home before heading with his wife to a gala to be held at the *Cercle L'Amicale*. He could not miss this opportunity to do business by meeting the Black elite who made up this prestigious club.

So, the two sisters remained alone that evening, sitting on the porch. Time-to-time Marie-Cécile's future plans and Marie-Agnès trip to Austria came up in their conversation. Yet, even though their exchanges were punctuated with humor and teasing, deep down, Marie-Agnès's mind was elsewhere. She was struggling with a growing need to know what was happening at the *Palmistes*.

Curiosity finally got the better of her. She got up to turn on the radio and tuned it on 4VRW radio. The enthusiasm of the commentator was on par with the historical moment.

"Seventy-two hours have already passed, dear listeners! There are only thirteen of them on the dance floor right now! Yes, thirteen couples! The end of this incredible competition is fast approaching! One of the sponsors is promising a true celebration of lights over the sea at the end of the competition! This celebration will offer the public a free, colorful fireworks display! Come see the final of this dramatic and exciting contest!"

"Oh my! Augustin and Christian are among the thirteen!" Marie-Cécile said energetically. "The crowd must be frenziedly stimulated! Let's go see!"

Marie-Agnès sensed her sister's excitement and desperately wanted to see Augustin. But two young girls, without a chaperon, leaving their house at nightfall to mingle with a throng of people at the city's waterfront was simply unthinkable.

However, instead of sharing her fears, Marie-Agnès heard herself say apathetically:

"Are you crazy? Calm down, my dear... This marathon is just another dance..."

Marie-Cécile grew impatient, irritated by her sister's persistence in trivializing the obvious.

"It's not just a dance, and you know it! He's doing it for you, to impress you!"

Troubled by Marie-Cécile's cutting insight troubled Marie-Agnès's eyes dilated, offended by the tone in which she was addressed.

"You don't know what you're talking about. The Sanatorium needs this money, and Augustin is a man of his word. He would never gamble with someone else's life..."

"Seriously?!" Marie-Cécile interrupted. "Augustin isn't just a man of his words; he's a man in love with you! Everyone knows that!"

"He won't be the last," Marie-Agnès replied without batting an eyelid.

"Stop fooling around... If you don't want him, then you'll end up losing him! "

Marie-Agnès suddenly felt anxious.

"What's wrong with you?!" she retorted, in a tone she intended to be ironic.

"You'll know what's wrong when you'll see her hanging on his arm..."

"What are you talking about?"

"You mean WHO am I talking about? It is Gisèle! She's in love with Augustin!"

A kind of fever shot like a rocket and flooded Marie-Agnès's cheeks, reaching her brain. Struck by a sudden palpitation, her vision blurred while everything around her was flickering.

In Augustin's heart, she taught, there was only room for her and her alone! Was she not his muse? Was she not the one who had the gift of making his grand ideas flourish? Was not it around her he always became the clumsiest and the most timid person?

Marie-Agnès stood up from her chair with a nervous energy, trying to hide the emotion she was struggling to contain. She rushed inside the house while she blurted out with a trembling voice.

"Who cares! So be it!"

CHAPTER 12
Eighty Hours…

That night, though a business meeting went longer than anticipated, Joseph Montrose, hurriedly, took the road toward the marathon. He wanted to witness for himself the results of his son's participation. It was past midnight and despite the late hour, a small group of spectators, enjoying the slow sounds of the orchestra, were watching the thirteen couples on the dance floor. Among them, some were speculating about who the grand prize winner would be.

"These people have completely lost it!" said one of them.

"Look at that participant and her number 27 on her back," replied another, his eyes narrowed, his finger pointing at Adrienne Dolan. "Since when women have that much strength?!"

"In my opinion, they're beyond crazy," added the friend who accompanied them. "Only a demon could have that kind of resistance."

"You're right! The chart on the podium shows eighty hours since she started dancing. It's unbelievable!"

While he was trying to locate Augustin on the dance floor, Mr. Montrose heard every word of their conversation. Surprised by their reasoning, he stared at them for a moment. To dismiss the participants' training, techniques, and endurance in favor of a demon shocked him deeply. He could not understand why the supernatural was so often put forward as an explanation for everything that eluded understanding.

Joseph Montrose was about to jump in the conversation when one of the marathon's coordinators spotted him. Mr. Carrey was coming along with the Director of Health and Human Services and a general practitioner.

"Montrose!" he blurted out. "I didn't expect to see you here so late! You came to support your son?"

"Yes... No doubt. I must report to his mother, you know," Mr. Montrose joked.

"Ah! So, he's the number 31," confirmed the general practitioner. "I saw your last name on the list of participants, but I made no connection..."

"That's him. Roger Grégoire's son is also in... But what about you? What are you two doing here?"

"We came to lend a hand to Dr. Wallon. We don't regret it because he was a little overwhelmed."

"Augustin and Christian are doing quite well," Mr. Carrey complimented. "If they hold on until the end, they could win on behalf of the country's tuberculosis patients."

"The Sanatorium is eagerly awaiting this donation. We are flooded by cases from working-class neighborhoods. And our small resources are dwindling by the day," said the Director of Health and Human Services in a confidential tone.

Joseph Montrose gasped. Any negative press due to tuberculosis could have a devastating effect on the tourism industry.

"If an epidemic breaks out, we're lost!" he said. "The rate of tourists visiting the country is currently among the highest in the Caribbean. We cannot let this kind of thing hinder the progress we're making."

"Don't worry. The Department of Public Health is very aware of this fact. And that's why we are multiplying prevention seminars," revealed the Director.

"You know, even if several medical students are providing support," informed the general practitioner, "we still have to pay medical staff, stock medicines, and increase the number of beds... So, we need funds to continue this fight."

"Augustin and Christian are determined! They'll win those 5,000 *gourdes*!" Joseph Montrose confirmed emphatically.

Mr. Carrey shook his head in approval while looking toward the participants.

"Yes, if they keep up the momentum, because all those who remain are just as determined..."

"They seem to be strong folks," added the Director of Health and Human Services. "The final hours will be tough..."

Despite the optimism of those staring at them, Christian and Augustin did not seem to be among the strong. Visibly exhausted, with dark circles under their eyes and slumped shoulders, they were suffering from a blatant lack of sleep.

Joseph Montrose said goodbye to his friends and moved closer. He flinched when he saw his son up close. Augustin was indeed pale. His unsteady legs forced him to lean on his partner. Mr. Montrose stared at him. He knew how crucial the final hours of a marathon could be, as exhaustion could mercilessly and suddenly take over body and mind.

Joseph Montrose looked around, searching for a way to help his son before it was too late. Augustin must not be eliminated or give up. His son was pushed by love. His resilience was proving it. Any defeat would crush his spirit.

Mr. Montrose rushed to the bar and ordered two cups of sweetened coffee, hoping the drink would be enough to revive his son. He blew on it to cool it down before hurrying back toward the dance floor.

He gestured several times to Augustin and Christian. Although they didn't understand the meaning of Mr. Montrose's gestures, the two friends slowly moved closer to him.

"Dad..." Augustin murmured feverishly, "we can't stop..."

"Drink this coffee," his father insisted. "Believe me, it will do you good..."

"We can't, Mr. Montrose," Christian interjected, equally exhausted. "We haven't even danced for an hour yet. We could be disqualified..."

"Especially since we only have two partners left."

"What happened to the third girl?" Mr. Montrose asked, surprised.

"Agathe wasn't feeling well... " Jocelyn started.

"She gave up," Augustin interrupted.

"So, more than ever, you need energy," Mr. Montrose concluded in a tone that no longer allowed for a reply. "Come get the coffee. There's no need to stop. Keep moving while drinking it!"

Augustin could barely bring the cup to his mouth. His hands shook it desperately. The fatigue was even felt in his throat; his tonsils seemed swollen, preventing him from drinking the liquid.

"Drink it all," his father insisted, his voice both firm and emotional. "You need strength. This check is important to your project."

Augustin exchanged a furtive, knowing glance with his father. Indeed, despite his physical condition, his determination had not faltered. His father reached out and touched his shoulder.

"You have no idea how proud I am of you," he said admiringly.

These words warmed Augustin's heart, so unaccustomed to such outpourings. His father's support made his feet light, giving him the desire to dream of victory. But soon, Mr. Gomez's voice brought him back to reality.

"And the competition continues! Thirteen couples are still on the dance floor! And yet there will only be one winner! Only one number can win the grand prize of 5,000 *gourdes*!"

"Number 28!" A group of young people fervently shouted.

"Number 24!" replied others opposite to them.

"No! Number 30!" argued a third group.

Joseph Montrose smiled, amused by their liveliness. So much energy coming from spectators in the prime of their youth reminded him of his own. There were those evenings when dancing and music had once been at the center of his life. A hint of nostalgia in his eyes, he turned back to his son to retrieve the cups.

"You only have a few hours left," he said, with pride in his voice. "I'll be back later today. Don't worry. You and Christian will make it! You can succeed!"

"Yes. We will. We will," Augustin repeated as if to convince himself.

Mr. Montrose made a gesture of victory, which, Augustin and Christian tried to return despite their fatigue. As Mr. Gomez thanked the many sponsors once again, Augustin's father left the club and headed home.

"We're at a crucial turning point in the marathon, ladies and gentlemen!", said Mr. Gomez. "There are only thirteen of them on the floor, thirteen brave couples who deserve to be introduced and applauded once again!"

As a wave of support erupted from the crowd, Mr. Carrey walked between the participants on the dance floor. Standing near each of them, he reintroduced numbers 5, 7, and 8 before letting the orchestra play. Then, bypassing Adrienne Dolan and her partner, he headed toward the Cantave children.

"Number 18, they are twins who are here to support the nation's industrial sectors of local merchants! We will never tire of thanking our Haitian entrepreneurs for their hard work and tenacity during the worst economic times!"

This announcement sparked an outburst of applause that surprised Emilio and his sister. The craze for consuming local products, which had begun during World War II, had not lost its momentum.

"Number 27 is currently the one and only female contestant. Her presence is an honor bestowed upon the female gender, which many wrongly consider the weaker sex! But number 27 is proving us wrong during this marathon!" Mr. Carrey said enthusiastically.

The women in the audience all rose to their feet to cheer Adrienne Dolan, drowning out the orchestra playing a bolero. The cries and shouts of admiration electrified everyone. This ovation made Emilia shudder as she watched the young woman adjusting slowly her large eye glasses. Adrienne was fixing the male competitors who were all looking at her. A slight smile of satisfaction and defiance lifted the corners of her lips.

"Numbers 30 and 31," Mr. Gomez continued, "are two friends participating for an extraordinary purpose, ladies and gentlemen! If they're here, it's not for their own pride! They're not here even for their own selfish gain! They are here doing this for the most vulnerable ones of our society. It's for tuberculosis patients who desperately need our care! Patients that need all of us! If they win the grand prize, they will donate all the funds to the Sanatorium of Port-au-Prince!"

A cry of astonishment shook the crowd, followed by an increasingly resounding ovation for Christian and Augustin. As the significance of their involvement became clear, some in the audience who had family or acquaintances with tuberculosis were unbelievably touched. A warm philanthropic sentiment permeated the crowd with the discovery of unselfish competitors dancing for a common good. Some were moved to tears because members from wealthy families finally cared about them.

They were lifting the veil on the pain, the struggles of the poor, the underprivileged.

Augustin and his friend bowed to the audience, with a hint of deep regret. If Mr. Montrose was still there, he would have been proud of them as he would witnessed the crowd's reaction.

The mention of numbers 32 and 46 went almost unnoticed, as the crowd erupted again at the introduction of the famous number 60. The shouts of Mayer's name came from every corner of the club.

Since they dined together on the night of the launch, Augustin did not pay much attention to him. He saw him as just another contestant. Despite the crowd's support, Max Belmont's departure ended up erasing the presence of number 60 in his mind. But with thirteen of them on this big dance floor, each competitor could now clearly see each other. Augustin felt that, facing Mayer's tenacity, he would have to draw on more energy if he wanted to win the grand prize.

Mr. Gomez and Mr. Carrey, smiled while trying to restore calm. The uproar took a while to subside as the introductions of numbers 50 and 95 completed the list of participants in the race.

Solon, number 95, let out a grin; he felt he merely inherited by default the applause that was directed previously toward number 60. Clifford F. Mayer indeed seemed stronger and more confident than he would ever be. Although he and Emilio were constantly monitoring him, Solon had the impression that the young man was keeping some of his techniques secret.

Yet, over the next few hours, Dr. Wallon's discerning eye began to detect signs of fatigue in Mayer. He ordered the young man to take a break to administer him an injection and an IV infusion.

Solon and Shilette, who were dancing nearby, did not grasped the medical jargon. All they heard was the word "injection." Solon wondered if he, too, should be asking for more vitamins. His shoulders were indeed sagging, and his posture was arching a little. He no longer had the strength to dance for six hours straight; but every three hours, he and Shilette took fifteen minutes to drink some water and wet their heads.

Shilette was dragging her feet even more than Solon. A nurse finally noticed her lack of energy and reported it to the doctor. Dr. Wallon approached immediately to examine the young girl. Shilette had a weak pulse, headaches, and a tingling sensation.

"Where are your parents?" the doctor asked.

"My mother isn't here..."

"We have a friend in the crowd," Solon corrected.

"Very well. I'm going to give you a treatment," the doctor said to the young girl. "If your body doesn't respond to it in a few hours, you'll have to stop."

Solon's heart pounded. With no other partner, it was out of question for Shilette to stop. Solon was not feeling as tired as she. Yet they have eaten the same food and have rested at the same time.

Reluctantly, Shilette was brought in. Assisted by a nurse, Dr. Wallon administered an IV. Shilette's eyes were bulging when she saw the syringes. She screamed, to the point that those around her began to mock her reaction.

"Calm down, miss!" the doctor begged. "It's for your own good that we're giving you these nutrients. After that, the nurse will give you a rubdown."

A quick glance at the contestants on the dance floor would have revealed that Shilette was not the only one losing energy.

As the hours were unfolding, the shouts and voices over the microphone grew weaker in Christian's ears. His heart rate was accelerating and his palms were sweating. Tension was building in his trapezius muscles, spreading to his lower back as his ankles grew heavy. His entire being demanded a rest he could no longer ignore.

"We're taking a break," he finally told Augustin. "We'll be back in ten minutes."

Visually exhausted, the partners separated. The girls dragged their feet heavy with fatigue, while rubbing their eyes, red from lack of sleep.

In the men's quarters, Augustin and Christian dropped themselves in the first empty chairs. Heads tilted back against a wall, they sat side by side, eyes closed, mouths open, barely able to speak to each other.

With each breath of air, a surge of pain gripped Christian's ribcage. He, who never wanted anything other than to have fun, felt a little uneasy. He opened his eyes and his gaze fell on Solon's camp bed. On it, he saw a bag containing the young man only change of clothes. The earlier image of a desperate Solon, forced to follow Shilette off the dance floor, filled him with self-disgust. He felt embarrassed, as if he was in their way; as if he no longer had a place in this marathon.

Christian searched for the right words, the best gentle sentences to convey to Augustin the decision he has made. The few moments he took to express them seemed to be an eternity.

“I'm out…” he finally blurted out without summary.

Augustin sat up suddenly, Christian's words took him by surprise, striking his ears violently.

“You not serious, right? What's happening to you? We're too close to the final! We can't give up now!”

“I'm tired and it's getting ridiculous,” Christian insisted through gritted teeth.

Augustin could not comprehend the words he heard. Everything he endured in the pursuit of this contest came flooding back to him: the disagreements with Mrs. Grégoire, the fear of losing Marie-Agnès, the days of uncertainty that distressed him...

“How will my father understand this desertion?” asked Augustin, still unable to forget his father’s gesture of victory. “He was just here this morning.”

“We're not going to kill ourselves, are we?” Christian asked impatiently. “We wanted to see if we could manage to dance for a hundred hours straight. We've lasted more than eighty, that's enough!”

“Our participation goes beyond a challenge! Human lives are at stake! If we win this money, it will go to the Sanatorium! Remember! All these suffering people need us!”

"They'll be taken care of... And besides, I didn't promise anything to them..."

"I did! I personally gave my word to the Sanatorium's director. I promised him we'd bring him that check! This isn't a joke. Our honor is at stake!"

Christian sighed, questioning in his mind why Augustin committed himself to this. He rubbed his forehead; scratched his head vigorously. Augustin's persistence was irritating him.

"Have you looked at Mireille and Jocelyn? They can barely stand up!"

"If we keep up, they'll keep going too..."

"They won't be able to..." Christian repeated slowly, emphasizing each word. "You want them to die on the dance floor? We don't even know their families!"

Augustin did not reply. His friend was right. Even though Jocelyn seemed to be the only girl who might make it to 100 hours, her increasingly cloudy eyes was not giving anyone much hope. Yet Augustin wanted to continue the gamble, drawing strength from his own reserves of determination.

"You can go then," he said sadly. "I'll keep the girls."

Christian burst into nervous laughter.

"They won't make it! They won't be able to last more than ten hours! Listen, we'll give them a little compensation and then we'll let it go."

Augustin fell silent. He was gradually realizing the extent of the shame he would face if he found himself without a partner before the end of the competition. Yet, even if he agreed to follow his friend in his withdrawal, it would be still a bitter failure.

A sudden feeling of anxiety seized Augustin. Desperate, he held his head in his hands as if to keep it from exploding. He had to find someone as quickly as possible: a relative, a friend, a stranger, anyone who would help him win the marathon!

The young man was on the verge of tears, the face of Marie-Agnès pierced the clouds in his mind. He had decided that the Sunday after he would win the marathon, he would go and reveal the burning flame that was consuming him. He had even chosen his jacket and the appropriate hat. He had found the words and rehearsed precisely a scene. He would arrive with a bouquet of softly colored roses. His act on behalf of tuberculosis patients would spread throughout the capital, even the entire country. He, Augustin, would be the one Marie-Agnès would want by her side.

"What will she think of me now?!" the young man blurted out in a broken voice.

Christian rolled his eyes. He needed to be done with this competition. His friend's fears were exasperating him, accentuating the fatigue he felt in his limbs.

"She'll never want a loser by her side! Never! And without Marie-Agnès, I'm lost!"

Annoyed, Christian stood up so violently from his chair that it tipped over.

"For God's sake, leave my sister alone!"

Augustin was speechless, sunken in his chair, taking the words like a slap in the face. Christian's shout turned heads, provoked whispers, and astonishment among those who admired their friendship for so many hours.

Augustin watched Christian gather his things while tearing off his back the number 30. With a distinct frustration in his face, the young man walked laboriously toward Mr. Gomez to announce his departure. Then, he headed toward the women's quarters and signaled to the girls to follow him before whispering a few words in their ears.

When the girls turned to look at Augustin, he realized that they, too, decided to abandon him. And Augustin Montrose, number 31, remained glued to his seat. For him, as for many other contestants, the dream was over. Hope faded without a second chance...

CHAPTER 13
Ninety Hours

The morning after this tragic episode, a few friends and neighboring store owners gathered in front of *Au Petit Dindon*. Everyone was following the progress of the contest from 4VRW radio. *Portail Saint-Joseph* was holding its breath at every broadcasted news.

Victorin was sitting on his familiar straw chair as two other store owners were sipping nervously some coffee Liliane just served them.

Standing near them in front of the counter, Béatrice was looking at the newspaper Alfred was reading, proud to have made the front page of a national newspaper.

"Oh! He left!" she said in amazement. "Clifford F. Mayer, the crowd's favorite? Wow!"

Victorin's anxiety suddenly vanished, replaced by a broad smile of relief.

"Really?" he said. "The favorite gave up from exhaustion this morning, and my children are still there!"

"He was too sure of himself," said Alfred. "His elimination doesn't surprise me at all."

"They said he was very experienced," Marguerite remembered.

"Exactly," Victorin added. "Experience is useful when you're humble. Age is a serious arbitrator that can claim its rights at any moment."

"You're right, my friend," said one of the merchants. "And it causes failures like this when you refuse to take it into account."

From inside the shop, Liliane leaned against the counter to read the newspaper Alfred was still holding.

"There are only ten of them now!" she exclaimed, her eyes glued to the paper.

"You know," said one of the store owners, "this contestant called Adrienne Dolan is something else! She's the one everyone's attention will be on now. I saw her in action the other day when I went to support Emilio. She's impressive."

"Yes," said Marguerite admiringly. "She's the favorite now. I must admit she surprised me too. I didn't think she'd make it this far. She already received numerous gifts and the support of many businesses. It wouldn't surprise me if she became the face of Bibby Soaps."

At her daughter's remark, *Madan* Vic, who was finishing her cup of coffee, poked her head over the counter door to point at Béatrice.

"Your sister right here deserves to be the face of big brands."

"Thanks, Mom," said Béatrice, blushing as she crossed her arms and tried to look taller.

"If only I could meet that photographer," her mother continued, "we'd thank him."

"Easy!" said one of the store owners. "Alfred just has to go to the newspaper office and ask for information."

Although she felt a little guilty for not having thought of it herself, Béatrice agreed it was an excellent idea. She instantly reviewed mentally the outfits she could wear to accompany Alfred. She imagined a short-sleeved dress, a large hat and matching heels, or simply a shirt with a high collar and a flared skirt that would reveal her thin waist.

Béatrice smiled mischievously as she took a cup of coffee from her mother. She first savored the coffee's vapors, thinking that her picture might be the catalyst for a new beginning. She sipped the brew, with a certain excitement in her heart. She would finally turn the page. Her simple career as a typist and stenographer would be over and her glamorous top-notched life as a model, that would be celebrated in fashion magazines spreads and advertisements, would begin. She would be the face of collections from New York as well as of the great cities of Europe. She would take her parents out of *Portail Saint-Joseph* and open a department store for them in one of those new two-story concrete buildings going up on the waterfront district. No more herring, no more bread trays, no more earthenware utensils. The selection would be nothing but European perfumes, crystal collectibles, fine linen, and fine jewelry...

While Béatrice was lost in her dreams and surrounded by people convinced of the imminent success of the Cantave twins, a few miles away, a tragedy was unfolding in the dining room of the Grégoire's family.

Slowly applying a spread on a piece of bread, Mrs. Grégoire's gaze was distant and worried. She could not wrap her mind around the fact that Christian abandoned the marathon. Her son appeared the day before on their porch like someone who escaped from prison. He was thinner, darker, with bushy eyebrows, and with an extremely wrinkled shirt. That morning, when Christian joined the rest of the family for breakfast, he had dark circles under heavy eyes.

Without any enthusiasm, he greeted everyone and chose what he wanted to eat: *akasan* (cornmeal beverage) and lightly buttered bread.

Mr. Grégoire and his wife remained silent, furtively examining the young man. They were holding back from exploding in anger. Yet, as soon as Christian put a piece of bread in his mouth, a barrage of questions came his way.

"I can't believe it," her mother said harshly. "So close to the goal and you gave up."

"And what did you do with your partners?" asked Marie-Agnès, who was putting salt on her boiled eggs.

"We hope you didn't send them away without compensation," her mother added.

A sad look on her face, Marie-Cécile suddenly stopped adding sugar to her cup of hot chocolate. She admired her brother so much that she felt his fatigue.

"Have pity of him, mom!" she cried.

When Christian returned from the contest, she was the first to rush over to him with a stool, raised his feet, and then massaged them with a bottle of Florida Water, hoping to relieve his pain. She was also the one who ordered the maid to bring him a cup of chamomile tea to soothe his emotional despair.

"We promised to pay them. But we haven't done so yet," said Christian.

Christian's answer annoyed his father. The young man was Mr. Grégoire's only son. He was the one whom all his hopes rested on; the right-hand man he needed to take the reins of his business. There was that vacation house he owned in *Canapé-Vert* and that he wanted to transform into a tourist lodge. Joseph Montrose and he discussed the project so many times before. They were at the stage where it was taking form. Mr. Montrose wanted to use the travel agency to feed the lodge with a steady stream of tourists. But Christian did not seem to be taking anything seriously; enjoying life at twenty-two years old was still his focus, the only thing that concerned him.

"I'll take care of that," Mr. Grégoire decided, dejected. "Anyway, Montrose contacted me last night. Augustin is devastated and he is worried about him."

Marie-Agnès jumped, causing her fork to fall to the floor.

"But why?" she asked, oblivious to the sound the utensil made as it hit the floor.

Christian lowered his eyes. He knew the reason for his friend's dismay. During a break, Augustin confessed the real motive for his participation. Yet, while this revelation did not surprise him, it did not change his own motivations either. He was there for the fun of it. The faint elusive pairing of fun and pain was finally obliterated under the weight of fatigue, provoking a fit of uncontrollable anger.

"Lasting more than two days in such a tough competition is a lot!" added Marie-Cécile.

"Huge!" her older sister realized.

Marie-Agnès paused. She wiped her lips, her face lighting up at the solution that came to her mind.

"Mom, we should invite Augustin to the house. We could gather a few friends to celebrate his courage and Christian's..." she suggested in a tone that barely concealed her excitement.

Mrs. Grégoire kept silent. She was assailed by frightening suspicions. With a frown on her face, she looked at Marie-Agnès with the same look she gave Augustin the day that, thanks to her maternal intuition, she realized that the young man was in love with her daughter. Augustin Montrose was probably adorable but he was not the man Elsa Grégoire wanted for Marie-Agnès.

For her two daughters rigorously raised according to the values and refinement of the Haitian elite, she wanted the best matches. Marie-Agnès was an accomplished pianist celebrated throughout the country. As a young woman of distinction, she needed a husband from an impeccable foreign family who would protect her from any financial worries. Maybe the son of one of the foreigners who were increasingly coming to live in the country would be perfect. Or at least the descendant of one of the European families who proved themselves in the Haitian society, just like her father, who came from Germany.

Therefore, Mrs. Grégoire who believed her daughter shared her values, was surprised by Marie-Agnès enthusiasm for this competition and wondered what she could find attractive about a walkathon. This little note that was inserted in the flowers on the evening of the recital at the *Rex Théâtre,* undoubtedly sparked something in her daughter's heart. Fortunately, Marie-Agnès was leaving soon for Austria. Mrs. Grégoire would arrange for her daughter to stay there as long as possible, ensuring that her connections in Europe would find for Marie-Agnès the right husband.

Elsa Grégoire had no intention of officially inviting Port-au-Prince's high society just for the mere son of a travel agency owner. She thus dismissed her daughter's suggestion with her silence.

For the moment, something terrible was worrying her. She was feeling a slight headache that was intensifying at the thought of public shame that her family would have to face. The whole city knew that her son was dancing for the benefit of the Sanatorium of Port-au-Prince; at the club *Cercle l'Amicale*'s reception, she and her husband received praises for such noble philanthropic leanings. And then there were also those articles published abroad that mentioned their surname. How could she and her husband now justify this withdrawal?

Elsa Grégoire was frightened at the thought that the gossip might have already begun. She squeezed her husband's arm convulsively.

"Roger, we have to do something! Whether we like it or not, we're all involved in this story. You can't just stand by and do nothing! We're heading straight for disaster!" she blurted out in a worried voice.

The words were coming out of Elsa Grégoire's mouth with a disconcerting speed. She was breaking out in cold sweat. Mr. Grégoire rubbed his forehead with his fingertips, irritated by his wife's skill of becoming alarmed at the slightest difficulty, letting her fear reach near hysteria.

With a raised eyebrow, Mr. Grégoire swallowed the last bite of his toast spread with *chadèk* (grapefruit) marmalade, then affectionately patted his wife's hand to soothe her.

"Calm down, my dear," he said after a moment of reflection. "We'll settle this matter quickly... Christian, you danced for three days straight, haven't you?"

"Yes," the young man replied wearily.

"Good... I'll speak to Montrose about donating to the Sanatorium on behalf of both our families."

Mrs. Grégoire stroked her husband's arm, her eyes full of admiration.

"Thank you, my friend! That will prevent us from looking like inept people!"

Christian's father wiped his lips, turning back to his son, clearly taking his time before speaking.

"Once this donation is made," he finally said, looking at his son in the eye, "you and I will have a little chat."

Christian's stomach knotted at the thought of this inevitable conversation. He knew that tone all too well. The last time he heard it, it was when he was studying in Switzerland and his grades were not what his father hoped for. When all of Europe was barely emerging from World War II, his father did not hesitate to reduce his financial support, forcing him to take a part-time job for a few months...

While Christian was mentally trying to figure out how to emerge unscathed from this tête-à-tête with his father, the battle for 5,000 *gourdes* was continuing in the *Palmistes* area.

Numbers 20, 53, and 65 voluntarily withdrew. The remaining couples were using tricks to stay in the race. Tired partners rested their heads on each other's shoulders, sleeping while the other continued to move. Others, having discovered, just like Solon, the closed-eye strategy, also begun to imitate him.

Yet, Dr. Wallon was vigilant. He never left the floor, watching for any sign of failings from the dancers. At regular intervals, he administered massages and vitamins to the ones who needed them. He did not hesitate to share his thoughts with the organizers on any competitor who did not take his advice seriously.

A strong sense of pressure was building up in the air, affecting the mood of the participants. Indeed, after Clifford F. Mayer's departure, Emilio and Solon were involuntarily watching each other; staring at each other like two men about to engage in an imminent swordfight. Gone were the extravagant choreographies and long conversations about their personal lives. They were looking at each other as if they were mutually mirroring their fatigue, their doubts, their worries.

Overwhelmed by exhaustion, Shilette could no longer hold back the tears that were streaming down her cheeks.

"Just a few hours, please," Solon kept whispering in her ear.

"I can't take it anymore!" the young girl sobbed.

"Just a few hours, please. That's all I ask, just a few more hours..."

"I want to go home..."

Solon was moving with the energy of a desperate man, reassuring himself with the thoughts of the hours that have already passed, of the sacrifices already made. His jerky movements were the opposite of Shilette's limp embrace. The firmer his grip, the looser Shilette's body became. The girl's knees were buckling under the accumulation of hours. Solon was doing everything he could to keep her in his arms, but the force of gravity was undeniably pulling them toward failure.

Abruptly, Shilette stopped complaining. The silence that followed was heavy on Solon's ears. Puzzled, the young man first looked at Shilette. Her eyes were closed. Her head tilted back. She was no longer moving. He whispered her name. She did not react. Her complexion was becoming increasingly gray.

Distressed, Solon frantically scanned the crowd, trying to find an explanation for what was exactly unfolding. But it was until his gaze met those of Emilio and his sister that he understood the magnitude of the situation. It was a disaster.

Struggling with the urge to rush to Solon, Emilio, his heart heavy, grinded his teeth in frustration. He knew such moved would mean the end for him as well. His heart pounding, he scanned the crowd, looking in vain for Alfred and Marguerite, hoping to beg them to come to the aid of his distressed friend.

"Lord!" Emilia cried out, worried by the sight of Shilette.

Rosa was watching, paralyzed. She grabbed her head and let out a cry of pain that shot through the crowd's heart. Cherilus and two other workers who were standing beside her pushed aside those in their path and rushed onto the dance floor. They barely caught Shilette as she was collapsing like a broken doll.

Dr. Wallon ran towards them, followed by the nurses and Mr. Gomez. He examined the girl where she fell and declared that she should not continue.

"Shilette… Shilette…" Solon screamed, but kept moving his feet.

Cries of fear, astonishment, and rage rose in waves from the spectators. They suddenly realized the depth of the exhaustion that was pressing down on the participants. The news of what just happened was propagated and exaggerated like the ripples on the surface of a pond. The spreading news was so distorted that some spectators heard a participant just fell dead.

Yet, Shilette did not passed away. She was still breathing. She was carried out on a stretcher. The instinct of motherhood overtook Rosa. She undid a checkered handkerchief holding her hair. She wrapped it tightly around her waist to gird her strength. A scream came out from the deepest corners of her soul. She threw herself on her daughter, unable to hold back her tears, uttered a series of wails.

“Don't worry,” Dr. Wallon tried to reassure her. “She just needs rest.”

Rosa wept even more as she felt helpless, shocked by the sight of her only child, lying flat on her back. It was only when Shilette moved her head and recognized her that the concerned mother calmed down a little.

But the lady merchant's sadness was soon lifted and her thoughts quickly shifted to their previously working plans. They were so close to the goal; the desire to open their own restaurant could not disappear with Shilette’s fainting. Desperate and unable to fully process what she just witnessed, Rosa turned her head back toward the dance floor with a somber face.

Yet, at the sight of Solon, still moving like a sleepwalker, her sorrow suddenly vanished. She jumped up from her daughter's bedside and hurried toward the dance floor. Her rushed steps broke one of her sandals, causing her to stumble. She abandoned them, and ran barefoot toward Solon. Her determination and her motherly devotion were transforming her into a warrior.

"Shillette... Shilette...," Solon kept repeating with a dying voice.

The young man was in a trance, internally leading a fierce struggle with reality. He was pacing in place. A complete fog seized his brain, wiping away the stubborn ambitions he harbored previously. The poshed *Bas-Peu-de-Chose* neighborhood where he dreamed of living was fading away into smoke. The small coffee business he envisioned was slipping into oblivion. He saw himself following a funeral procession where the deceased were his parents, his brothers, his sisters. They were all buried in the dried fields of *Jérémie*. He found himself alone on an imaginary sailboat in the middle of the sea, under a deadly sun, heading into exile to an unknown kingdom.

Solon's eyes were bulging out as a chill ran through his entire being. He whispered imperceptibly and disjointedly, a few verses by Etzer Vilaire, a famous poet from his town of *Jérémie*:

> *"Life is sad, yes! But it is of a certain magnificence.*
> *It is a sublime instinct this strange persistence*
> *To fight, to hope, to love, to be, and to believe*
> *In an eternal dream of splendor and triumph..."*

Rosa looked at Solon for a split second; she did not understand a word he was muttering. She grabbed him and shook him. Fear and urgency in her voice, she uttered a barrage of offensives words typical of the region of *Cayes-Jacmel,* hoping to wake him up.

Taller than her, the young man was looking straight above the lady merchant's head; he was still reciting the poem. His weight, as the minutes passed, was becoming too much for her.

"For your own good," she said in a savage tone, "You better keep on dancing! Because if you fall on me, I'll give you a *palavire* (a strong slap) that will send you all the way to your family in *Jérémie*!"

A cheer from the crowd greeted Rosa's entrance. Surprised by the audience's reaction, the lady merchant grimaced. Emanating the smell of the food she sold that day, sweat oozed from the roots of her braided hair, trickling down her face and neck. The crowd was getting fond of her. Feeling more relax, she attempted unsuccessfully to hum along with the music that was playing.

The tragedy that was unfolding did not escape the musicians of the *Orchestre Caraïbes* either. Under the direction of the organizers, they began to play lively in the hope of distracting the crowd from the distressing scene.

The melody of the trumpets could be heard for miles around. The announcements from the 4VRW commentator encouraged even more people to come see the finalists. But Rosa was no dancer. The entire crowd could attest to that. She was one of those women who would not let herself be led. Her body's stiffness was evident in the contraction of Solon's muscles, who had to counteract her jolts. Even so, he was dragged from side to side so he would not collapse.

Yet Solon was not falling. His feet felt strange. He felt the cement floor as if he was barefoot. Puzzled, he lifted one of his shoes, and noticed with horror that the sole had a hole in it.

CHAPTER 14

And The Hundredth Hour arrived...

On the last day of the 100-Hour Grand National Dance Marathon, dusk was already falling on Port-au-Prince. The tempered air was brought on by a breeze coming down from *Morne l'Hôpital*. Christian's parents, joined by Mr. Montrose, were at a hotel grand opening. Their children were left without any specific plan for the evening.

The calm in the *Bois-Verna* neighborhood was making Christian restless. For the past three days he grew accustomed to the incessant rhythms of the contest. Now, it was all gone. The young man was repeatedly glancing anxiously at the living room clock and was internally counting the passing minutes and hours. The pendulum's balancing movements twisted his stomach into a knot. He felt an unbearable discomfort. He was frantically tapping the end of a pen on a small table. The noise was irritating his sisters who sat across from him in rocking chairs, their shawls wrapped around their shoulders.

To their relief, Christian stood up, walked a pace, and leaned against the gallery's lacework balustrade. As he watched a few fireflies illuminate the lawn with their soft, flickering light, he felt the coolness of the night on his skin. He ran a hand over his forehead, letting it slide to the center of his skull. Solon's voice was echoing in his head, adding to a sort of an undefined distress.

Christian was now leaning against a post of the balustrade; lost in his own mind, he paid little attention to his sisters exploding into bursts of laughter. Dressed as they all were, you would have thought that they were welcoming governmental officials. It has been a while since the girls were being entertained loudly by clumsy stories of one of Marie-Cécile's suitors.

However, Christian's serious face did not escape Marie-Agnès. She gave him a questioning gaze. He acceded to her inquiry.

“You know, girls, there's a guy in the marathon, number 95… I've never seen someone with such determination...” the young man finally confessed.

“What family is he from?” asked Marie-Agnès.

“I don't think we know them. He’s from *Jérémie*… I don't even remember his name.”

"So, what's bothering you so much?" Marie-Agnès replied, shrugging her shoulders casually.

Christian was searching his own thought for an answer and was fixing the ground.

"I would love for him to be the winner..." he finally admitted.

'I have plans', he remembered number 95 saying. This simple answer from Solon never left Christian, giving way to a gamut of suppositions from economic to social. The minimum national wage was 1.50 *gourde* ($0.30 USD). Four days of dancing meant 6 *gourdes* ($1.20 USD) lost when no one knew who would win. This young man surely had to pay rent and a family to support, or other dire obligations, and then... 'the plans'...

"I have to go see!" Christian said resolutely. He threw his jacket on and started to depart.

Marie-Cécile jumped to her feet.

"I'll go with you!"

"Are you coming too?" Christian asked his older sister.

Without hesitation, Marie-Agnès nodded. She may not have known the remaining competitors, but her sister and Christian's enthusiasm was contagious. Besides, for a while now, deep down, she has been looking for an excuse to see Augustin. While she was embarrassed to ask her brother to bring him over, she also did not want to go to him without a reason that would not arouse suspicion.

"First, I'd like us to go to Augustin's house," the young lady heard herself say in a tone she intended to be casual.

Marie-Cécile's eyes widened in surprise. She stared at her sister, who was trying to avoid her gaze.

Unaware of the reason for this whish, Christian looked annoyed. He has not yet settled his disagreement with Augustin.

"Why?" he asked. "We have no need to go there."

Startled, Marie-Agnès, stared at her brother and noticed his embarrassment.

"What do you mean?" she asked. "Don't tell me you two had a falling out?"

Christian looked at the clock and grew impatient.

"Are you coming with us or not?"

Eating up by curiosity, Marie-Cécile seconded her sister's wish.

"I'm sure we'll have time to quickly pass by the Montrose's house!"

Marie-Agnès got out of her rocking chair and stood before her brother.

"You were practically born at the same time. I don't see what disagreement could break this brotherly bond. You couldn't continue dancing because you were tired, and that's all," she insisted.

Christian knew that was not all. But he did not feel the need to argue. Without adding anything, he picked up his hat while Marie-Cécile was fixing her shawl.

Marie-Agnès quickly went up to her room with the sole intention of getting gloves and also a hat. But she stopped in front of the mirror on her dresser and inspected herself from head to toe. She smoothed the flared of her leaf-green dress, adjusted the round collar, inspected the white buttons that were lining up along one side. She picked up a black belt that matched her accessories but quickly abandoned it. She tied her hair in a bun, then let it down, then another bun. She changed her shoes several times and was about to put on some blush when her impatient brother startled her from downstairs. Marie-Agnès took a deep breath before leaving her room. Her face was stiff with the rising tension.

At her sister's sight, a slight smile tugged at the corners of Marie-Cécile's lips, while keeping for herself all the questions racing through her mind.

The siblings hurried down the front steps of the house, walking speedily toward the street. The moon was half-visible, guiding them with a faint light. They were walking side by side without saying a word, each one's heart beating at the rhythm of different reasons.

Christian was about to confront his best friend for the first time since the night of disagreement. Marie-Agnès was searching for the right words, refusing to admit why she was going to such great lengths to find them. Meanwhile, Marie-Cécile, following them almost at a gallop, was eager to discover the real reasons that pushed her sister to stop at Augustin's house first.

Christian pushed open the small gate of the house and let his sisters go in first. Marie-Agnès went ahead, filled with a sudden courage. The further in she walked, the more the large bougainvillea in front of the house seemed to point to the right direction, the way to the porch.

Sitting in a corner, Augustin was barely visible in the twilight. In the background, behind him, all the living room's jalousie doors were open. Only a dim lamp was illuminating a record player from which was coming a melancholic rendition of an Opus from Chopin.

Marie-Agnès swallowed her saliva, each musical line conveying to her the depths of the young man's despair.

Augustin heard footsteps on the gravel, but made no effort to look towards the gate's entrance. Soon, the three intruders were at the bottom of the stairs; and in the dim evening light, Augustin saw the flared skirt of a young woman who was purposeful climbing the steps. The hourglass figure of the woman accentuated the mystery of the lady.

He closed his eyes for a moment, convinced deep down that it could never be Marie-Agnès. Christian convincingly destroyed any hope he had. But now, it is only days before his beloved departs for Austria. His failure in the marathon erased even the slim idea of a future together. Her heart must be elsewhere. She must despise even the mentioning of his name...

Augustin closed his eyes for a moment and opened them wide realizing something. This silhouette! That pace! It was Marie-Agnès's gait and her perfume floated towards him! No, he was not dreaming! He stood abruptly from his chair. He hastily patted his face, trying to erase the dark circles under his eyes cause by so many tears.

Marie-Agnès trembled. She had never seen Augustin in such state of neglect. His beard was full and unkept and his eyes frighteningly blurry. As she was getting closer, she was desperately fighting the growing urge to take Augustin in her arms and console him.

"A Mozart would be better suited for the circumstances than this study of Chopin," she said in a calm and gentle voice.

Augustin's eyes were wild and confused. This unannounced apparition left him stunned; his ears were ringing with words of his beloved. Sweat trickled down the middle of his back; and he felt hot as his clammy hands trembled.

Marie-Agnès moved even closer; though, stressed, shivering, and squeezing her own fingers frantically.

"Everything's okay? We haven't seen much of you in the last few hours..."

Heavy-tongued, Augustin's dazed gaze swept over those accompanying the young lady. He was slowly returning to a kind of reality that caused rapid heartbeats and intake of air. All the resentment from the evening when Christian abandoned him was rising within him. The few hours separating them from victory did not weigh heavily on that decision. If only they were resilient then, tonight, he would have been a happy man...

Augustin's jaw tightened, looking away at the same time as Christian. He raised his head and cleared his throat.

"Uh... Yes, yes. I'm fine," he replied, his tone intended to be casual. "I was tired... I needed to rest."

"We understand... You deserve it... We're so proud of you..."

With a trembling smile on his lips, Augustin breathed deeply. He was staring at Marie-Agnès as if trying to engrave in his memory an image he was seeing for the last time. Heat consumed his cheeks and his stomach tightened and tingled…

Christian glanced furtively at his best friend and finally realized the depth of his feelings for his sister. And all things considered, he would have much preferred him to the pretentious men who hovered around Marie-Agnès and who did not share her dreams…

Christian was bothered by his reaction toward Augustin. He felt sorry for hurtful words he did not mean. Despite the tension in the air, remorse was evident on his face.

"I'm sorry for what I said to you... I'm sure exhaustion had a lot to do with it..."

The two sisters looked at each other, completely oblivious to what their brother was referring to.

"Perhaps you already know," he said as he shoved his hands in his pockets, puffing out his chest. "Our parents have decided to make the donation to the Sanatorium anyway..."

Augustin remained silent. It was not charity he was begging for when he decided to enter the competition. He was seeking recognition from the woman he loved deeply. He wanted to win her heart. He wanted to pay for it with his very self and any sacrifices that he knew that no other man in her circle would ever have made...

By the way Augustin's lips dropped, Marie-Agnès heard his silence: he was a proud man. Her admiration for him quintupled in just a few seconds. She was now physically very close to the young man. Her mind no longer controlling her words, she gave free rein to her heart.

"You know, to have lasted so long in this marathon, it's extraordinary!" she declared passionately. "The two of you drew considerable attention to tuberculosis, a disease no one wanted to talk about. You highlighted this institution that few people cared about. You gave a voice to these unfortunate people. Do you realize that?!"

Augustin was speechless, lapping every word coming from Marie-Agnès. His eyes shone, his face contorted, his hands froze by the emotion he was trying to hold back. Internally, he was being driven mad with joy.

The voice of Marie-Agnès was growing thin under the pressure of her heart.

"We're here because we wanted you to know... Well... I wanted you to know that I'm particularly touched by your generous heart. You're a worthy man, Augustin!"

Trembling, Marie-Agnès lost totally her composure after her heartfelt words. It was for the first time in her life she had such warm feelings toward a man. She breathed deeply, trying to calm herself down while Augustin was losing control.

He threw himself at the feet of Marie-Agnès, grabbed her hands and pressed them to his tear-soaked face. He was shaken to his core. Caught off guard by the sensation of Augustin's lips on her skin, Marie-Agnès shuddered, overcome by a wave of emotions.

"If only you knew how much I love you!" Augustin finally blurted out.

Christian and Marie-Cécile were caught up in this scene despite themselves. They were stunned by the fearlessness Augustin was putting forth and the reciprocal feeling Marie-Agnès was showing. Their usually self-contained sister was yielding to her conceal affection.

Marie-Cécile was listening intently, speechless in front of this passionate exchange. She was wondering how

Marie-Agnès could have kept her feelings so hidden from her for so long. The young girl had a wild urge to give a round of applause; imagining Giselle Volmar's reaction to this developing relationship.

Christian crossed his arms behind his back, admiring the tips of his shoes, his face lit up by his friend's happiness.

"You see," he teased, a half-smile on his lips. "You wouldn't have heard all those beautiful words if we'd died..."

Marie-Cécile burst out laughing while admiring Marie-Agnès and Augustin wiping each other's eyes, lost in their own world. The gong of the wall clock in the living room echoed through the night, bringing them all back to the reason they wanted to go out in the first place.

"Oh, no! We're about to miss the final," exclaimed Marie-Cécile.

"We have to go," hurried Christian. "The contest ends tonight! Would you like to come with us, Augustin?"

Augustin nodded yes.

"Give me a few minutes, though," he asked with pleading eyes.

As soon as Augustin left, Marie-Cécile leap at her sister's neck, who in turn hugged her, squealing with joy. With a knowing look, Christian shared their happiness while deep inside of him, he was already amused at their mother's reaction, when she will soon discover there was no hope of future between Marie-Agnès and any Francini.

Augustin rapidly came back, changed, clean-shaven, hair tamed. The blissful glow emanating from him transformed him so much so that Marie-Agnès's heart leaped at his sight. Augustin took the young lady's hands and kissed them deeply.

"Come on, lovebirds! Let's go!" said Christian, pulling them apart.

Marie-Agnès went down the steps, clinging to her sister's arms, overcome with a euphoria she never believed existed. She was walking as if on cloud nine, right in front of Augustin, who could not take his eyes off her.

Christian noticed it and gave him a hug in silence.

"I still don't know what you see in her," he teased quietly.

"She's a rare pearl, a finely polished diamond. The treasure I've always sought..." Augustin whispered.

Marie-Agnès blushed and giggled with her sister, walking briskly toward the *Champ de Mars*. Hearing Augustin's voice finally giving life to what she had always suspected filled her with pure jubilation.

"Once we will be at the waterfront, we should stay for the fireworks," suggested Marie-Cécile who wanted to see some enchantments in this evening full of revelations.

"Unfortunately," replied Augustin, "the fireworks are scheduled for tomorrow at the opening of the official section of the International Exhibition, and also for Tuesday. My father received invitations with reserved seats for the last evening. It will be over the sea, at the *Palmistes*. We could all go then."

Marie-Agnès suddenly felt the urge to attend the show alongside Augustin. She did not want to miss this display of light which promised to be one of the most beautiful and the largest ever seen in Haiti. She looked imploringly at her brother, who understood that she needed a chaperone.

"Good idea," he said with a wink and a mischievous smile.

The little group now just crossed the *Grand-Rue* Street. The number of passersby was increasing and the music of an orchestra was getting closer and louder. They were not far from the club.

"Do you remember the guy who was number 95?" Christian asked his friend.

Augustin tried to recalibrate his thoughts while he could not take his eyes off Marie-Agnès.

"Uh… Yes, yes! The one who accidentally hit me on the first night?"

"Right!"

"What's wrong with him?"

"He's competing for some projects he wants to carry out," Christian explained as if he had known Solon forever.

"Let's hope he's still there," Marie-Cécile anticipated thoughtfully.

"Even if he doesn't win," Marie-Agnès said with a worried expression, "we'll try to find out who he is. We'll help him..."

Moved by his lady's selfless idea, Augustin smiled, poking fun at himself a little. His father was right. What he thought was a failure was the key to the heart of the woman he adored. She was one of those women of conviction who was only impressed by unparalleled devotion. He waited for this moment for so long and it finally arrived. They were in perfect harmony.

The access to the club was difficult. A long line of people was standing in the front, waiting to enter. Despite the admission for this last night climbed to 3 *gourdes* ($0.60 USD), the club was packed. The little group of friends could hardly make their way through the dense and agitated crowd. Unable to take two steps without bumping into someone, a little startled Marie-Agnès clung to Augustin's arms while holding her sister's hand.

"Sorry," apologized Christian, who in passing bumped unexpectedly into Shilette.

Shilette regained some strength and was standing with Cherilus. Without saying a word, she watched the group pass behind her, then turned and continued to shout her support for Solon.

Despite the colorful scarf expertly wrapped around her head, Christian recognized the girl's big eyes, her rounded face, and her dimples. He shuddered, disconcerted by her presence in the crowd and not on the dance floor.

"But you're number 95's partner!"

"Oh, no!" Augustin exclaimed. "You were eliminated?!"

It took Shilette a while to realize who was standing behind her.

"No, sir. He's not eliminated. He's there!" she said with a shy voice, pointing her finger at Solon.

Heart pounding, Christian followed the direction indicated and saw Solon, covered in sweat, visibly on the verge of a seizure.

"There he is!" he said to his sisters. "He's number 95!"

"Unbelievable!" Augustin snapped.

"Go number 95!" Marie-Cécile screamed.

Head thrown back, Solon heard the screams as distant noises. He seemed to be unaware of his partner; his arm was no match for Rosa's relentless efforts. The number 95 was still shining on the back of his crumpled and dirty clothes. The point of one of his shoes was crumbling. His feet were dragging even more on the ground.

As for Rosa, her sleepy eyes were barely remaining open. The lady merchant was collapsing from exhaustion. When she replaced her daughter on the dance floor, she never once imagined how hard participating in this dance marathon would be. Just like Shilette, she barely ate, drank a little, nor slept. She was wearing the same clothes from the previous evening, becoming thus a show within a show for spectators looking for an uncommon thrill.

A few laborers and gardeners that Solon was acquainted with agreed to take some of the money they were saving for rent, for food, or to pay off their debts, to come see with their own eyes this finale, impressed by how far Solon's unfailing determination had taken him.

Not far away from them, Alfred, Liliane, and Marguerite were also there to support the twins. Victorin was feeling particularly weak that evening; *Madan* Vic decided to stay and take care of him. This unexpected opportunity suited Victorin. He wanted to discuss with his wife the pick-up truck he intended to acquire. He then encouraged Béatrice to go along with her siblings.

The young woman readily accepted, this time with the firm resolution to make her dreams come true, eliminating from the outset any possibility of returning home without securing a chance to leave for Paris...

A little before 11:00 p.m., just as the number of attendees was reaching its peak, Mr. Carrey, covered in sweat, picked up the microphone.

"And 100 Hours has just been completed, ladies and gentlemen!"

"Good God!" shouted Mr. Gomez. "What stamina! These ten competitors are among the most resilient we've ever seen!"

The entire crowd let out a unanimous "hurrah" that rocked the club.

"Go number 95! Go!" shouted Christian and Augustin, while Marie-Cécile was jumping up and down with excitement.

Marie-Agnès put her hands over her ears, stunned, frightened, horrified. She was not accustomed to this uncontrolled outpouring of energy and enthusiasm. Yet, beside her, a young woman wearing a simple white blouse and a brick-colored pencil skirt was standing serenely, her eyes fixed on a particular dancing couple. Marie-Agnès noted her expertly arranged curls, her lipstick precisely applied, her hazel eyes barely outlined. Her face seemed familiar, as if she met her before at a show or by a hotel pool, if not at a dance party at the prestigious *Cabane Choucoune…*

"I feel like we know each other, if I'm not mistaken," Marie-Agnès finally said, curiously.

Béatrice turned toward the voice and noted the subtle perfume, the matching accessories, the perfectly styled bun.

"No, I don't think so," she replied calmly.

"Ah, sorry…"

Marie-Agnès confusion aroused suspicion in Béatrice, who tried to understand her disappointment. Suddenly, a slight smile played on Béatrice lips. Surely the woman standing next to her has seen a photo of her and she was impressed.

"No, it's fine," said Béatrice. "Perhaps you've seen me in the newspapers."

"Ah!" said Marie-Agnès, now a little bit curious. "That's right... I'm Marie-Agnès Grégoire. Pleased to meet you."

Béatrice first looked at the hand Marie-Agnès held out to her. A hand with long fingers and manicured nails that strangely resembled an open door to her dreams of grandeur. The young woman shook it without hesitation.

"Marie Béatrice Cantave. Please to meet you."

The family name intrigued Marie-Agnès. She remembered a Mr. Cantave, also of German descent. He was once her father's right-hand at the Department of Finance. Béatrice seemed to have inherited the features of this notable economist; a man who left his mark on the Haitian financial sector. Marie-Agnès would have liked to know more about the young woman, but the setting was not favorable. Caught up in the mingling of the orchestra's music and the commotion of the crowd, the two women looked at each other for a moment and exchanged a suppressed smile before turning their head back towards the dance floor.

They were breathing in unison, patiently waiting for the marathon to end. They would not lose sight of each other. Marie-Agnès needed to count, as she believed, this relative of Mr. Cantave among her circle of friends; just as much as Béatrice was curious to discover how far the impression left by her photograph would bring her.

Standing near their sister, the rest of the Cantave children was shouting their support to the point of losing their voice. Emilio and Emilia must be the winners, and every shout they let out was a reminder of their duty.

Emilio Cantave never abandoned this mission, despite his number 18 hanging miserably on his back. Sweat was trickling down his face; his shirt was soaked and clinging to his chest. Although exhaustion was heavy, he kept on pushing himself hard, constantly counting the number of competitors.

They were ten.

Ten couples for 5,000 *gourdes* ($1,000 USD).

Ten couples who had all exceeded the 80 hours required to split the cash.

Emilio frowned.

There was no feat in receiving just 500 *gourdes* ($100 USD). The mere thought gave him a surge of energy.

"Come on, Lia," he said to his sister. "We're almost there. Hang in there."

Emilia was resting both of her hands heavily on her twin's shoulders, her mouth open, trying to fill her lungs with air. At times, she clenched her teeth from the pain causing by cramps in her feet and calves.

The marathon, for her too, was becoming a torture. She looked up at her brother with dull eyes, barely bearing the blisters on her aching feet. A slight dizziness was seizing her. She was surprised to still be there. She, too, must have Adrienne Dolan's strength and valor.

Indeed, Adrienne Dolan, number 27, was still dancing. Her clothes were creasing; her eyes were diming; and every movement was becoming a heavy chore. But the fight was not over as she was surrounded by numbers 5, 7, 8, 24, 32, 46, and 50. For anyone watching, her resilience was a miracle. Crowds of women were there only to admire her; they endeavored to comprehend her determination to triumph; they wanted to understand her stoic face behind her large dark eye-glasses frame.

"103 hours, ladies and gentlemen!" announced one of the commentators of 4VRW radio.

"103 hours since they started dancing under these palm trees!" the other observed. "They're exhausted, but they're not giving up!"

"We're in the final minutes! Maybe the final seconds! The coordinators aren't allowing any more breaks! It's now non-stop! At any moment, we could have a winner!"

"But who will win, ladies and gentlemen?! Who?!"

"Hurry up and join us at the *Palmistes* and see for yourself who will win the 5,000 *gourdes*!"

The crowd was hysterical, breathless, impatiently waiting for the step that would break everything; that final step that would lead to victory for a single couple.

But, on the dance floor, between the nightclub's tall palm trees, amidst the incessant shouts, a peculiar kind of dance was taking place as the hands of the clock was turning. A dance where mechanical movements were not following the rhythm of the *Orchestre Caraïbes*.

Emilio and Emilia could no longer take their eyes off Solon and Rosa. Each passing minute was felt like a tear in their legs and feet. However, their limbs were still putting a resistance against the fatigue.

Their eyes were sparkling with a new flame, silently exchanging a profound message. Their bodies were now moving in the same direction, surrendering to the tyranny of bonds created.

They will not give up on themselves.

They will not give up on their dreams…

ABOUT THE AUTHOR

Pascale Doxy is an author and an artist known for her compelling narratives and often intricate artwork. Her artistic journey began at a young age, nurtured by prestigious mentorships and self-directed learning, culminating in numerous exhibitions throughout the United States.

Her historical novels transcend time, revealing forgotten eras of Haitian history and seamlessly blending everyday Caribbean life with the rich past and enduring mysteries of Haiti.

Print in the United States by Lulu Press, Inc.

www.ingramcontent.com/pod-product-compliance
Lightning Source LLC
LaVergne TN
LVHW020536100826
845148LV00010B/1484
* 9 7 9 8 2 1 8 9 4 5 4 4 2 *